KISS THE SKY

HER ELEMENTAL DRAGONS BOOK TWO

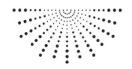

ELIZABETH BRIGGS

ISBN (paperback) 9781724368164

ISBN (ebook) 9781948456029

www.elizabethbriggs.net

For all the men who stand beside us as we save the world

1

KIRA

Fire burst into life inside my open palm, and with it came the fear. I forced myself to keep the flame going and to stare at the ball of light and heat in my hand, even as cold terror washed over me and sent shivers down my spine. For much of my life fire had been my torment and my terror, a reminder of my past and a deadly threat to my future, but not anymore. Now I was going to learn to control it—and my fear with it.

"Are you trying to kill us all?" a cold voice asked behind me.

I turned toward Reven, squinting against the bright sun behind him. "I need to practice if I ever want to get better with fire."

"Not on this boat." My black-haired assassin gestured around us. "This entire thing is made of wood. One stray spark and we'll all go up in flames."

He did have a point. I closed my hand over the ball of fire, immediately dousing it. "It's a good thing we have you then, isn't it?"

He scowled, but it didn't make him any less handsome. If anything, quite the opposite. "Nice to know my role in this group is to keep you and Jasin from burning the world down."

He shot a glare at Jasin, who stood on the other side of the boat talking with Auric while making flying gestures with his hands. Auric's golden hair caught the sunlight while he crossed his arms and furrowed his brow at whatever Jasin was saying. My fourth mate, Slade, sat nearby, ignoring the two of them as he sharpened his axe. He had the rich, dark skin common in the Earth Realm, along with a short beard and a large, impressive body that was all muscle.

"Your role in this group can be whatever you wish," I said. "Assuming you actually want to be one of us, that is."

"I'm here, aren't I?" Reven snapped, before spinning on his heel and stalking off, his black cloak trailing behind him. I sighed as I watched his brooding form disappear below deck. He was here, yes. But would he stay this time?

I leaned on the wooden railing and gazed across the waves. An unnatural wind—created by Auric—tousled my hair and filled the sail, guiding our boat northeast toward the Air Realm. In every direction all I saw was water and sky, a never-ending field of varying shades of blue that reminded me of my childhood spent in the Water Realm. After years living in the other kingdoms I only now realized how much I'd missed being surrounded by the ocean. I wondered if

Reven felt the same, since he'd also grown up in the Water Realm, but I doubted he would admit it to me if he did.

I rarely thought about my childhood since it only brought pain, but now I closed my eyes and breathed in the salty air and let my mind travel back. Back to growing up on the shoreline under the shade of palm trees. Back to the smell of fresh fish off the boat. Back to my mother, with her hazel eyes and sandy hair, and my father, with his scratchy beard and sun-kissed skin. The Fire God had told me they weren't my birth parents, but to me they always would be my real family. Besides, I looked nearly identical to my mother, except I had red hair instead of blond. How could she not be my real mother? And if they weren't my birth parents, then who was?

Perhaps the Air God could tell me once we made it to his temple. This was only our first full day on this boat— we'd spend last night either trying to figure out how to sail, or passed out from exhaustion after our encounter at the Fire Temple—but we had many more days ahead of us before we would reach the Air Realm and the temple there. And after that our journey would continue across the other Realms, growing more impossible with each day.

For hundreds of years our world had been ruled by the five Dragons, the divine representatives of the Gods of earth, air, fire, water, and spirit. But in recent years the Gods had grown weary of the Dragons' oppressive control and recently chose new Dragons to take their place: me and my four mates. Only problem? The current Dragons had no interest in stepping down.

For most of my life I'd rarely spared a moment to think on the Gods, absent as they were, and when I thought of the Dragons it was with fear and anger. All of that changed on my twentieth birthday when I was struck by lightning and began having visions of the four men who would become my mates. A month later they each arrived in my village and I was forced to face the truth: that I was the next Black Dragon, who represented the Spirit Goddess and could control all five elements. The other men—Jasin, Slade, Auric, and Reven—each represented one of the other elements. And to unlock our powers and our Dragon forms, I had to bond with all of them.

Yesterday I'd bonded with Jasin, my confident, flirtatious soldier, who'd been chosen by the Fire God to be the next Crimson Dragon. Jasin had once served the current Dragons in the Onyx Army, but he'd had a change of heart after he was forced to do things he didn't agree with, including wiping out entire villages thought to be harboring members of the Resistance. At first I'd been hesitant to give my heart or my body to Jasin since he was a complete stranger to me, although not to other ladies it seemed. But after ten days of traveling to the Fire Temple together he'd won me over and I'd eagerly taken him as my mate.

The memory of it sent a rush of warmth through me now. His hands on my skin. His mouth between my thighs. The fire that had swept over us as the bond had completed. And when it was done, I'd been able to summon fire and Jasin could turn into a dragon.

Next I was meant to bond with Auric, my thoughtful,

clever prince, who would represent the Air God as the Golden Dragon. He'd left behind his life as a royal and a scholar to be at my side, and I'd already come to value his kindness and intelligence. We were traveling toward the Air Realm now, where his parents ruled, though I wasn't sure what we would encounter there. Auric had sneaked away to be with me, and I had a feeling his family wouldn't be pleased with him. After Jasin's family betrayed us to the Onyx Army, it didn't seem wise to tell anyone else who or what we were. Either way, I was looking forward to bonding with Auric at the Air Temple, especially when I remembered his kisses, which had left me wanting even more.

Slade would be my next mate after Auric, though he didn't seem happy about that fact. He'd once been a humble blacksmith—although one who had connections with the Resistance, it seemed—before the Earth God had selected him to become the Jade Dragon. Slade hadn't wanted to leave his old life behind, and I got the feeling there was a woman in his past that was part of that, but I'd never once questioned his loyalty. I just wasn't sure if we'd ever have the kind of relationship I had with Jasin and Auric. Sometimes Slade looked at me in a way that made me think he desired me as much as I did him, but then he would turn away and the moment would be lost. I could only hope he would open up to me by the time we reached the Earth Temple.

Reven, on the other hand, had made it clear from the start he didn't want to be the next Azure Dragon, and didn't care one bit that the Water God had chosen him. Despite the undeniable chemistry between us, he'd resisted me and pushed me away at every turn. In the Fire Realm he'd eventually left us all behind, saying he wanted no part of our journey anymore and that caring for people made one weak. He'd returned a day later and saved my life, but I wasn't sure I could ever trust him again after he'd left us when we needed him most. But I'd have to find a way, because eventually we'd have to bond in the Water Temple too.

No matter what challenges we faced, I needed to take all four men as my mates to gain all of their elemental powers and become the next Black Dragon. Only then could we stop the current Dragons—and take their place as the protectors of the world.

"All right, I'm going to try it," Jasin said, his voice carrying over on the wind and interrupting my thoughts.

"Are you sure this is wise?" Auric asked, his brow furrowing.

Slade shook his head. "You're going to get yourself killed."

Jasin waved their concerns away. "I've got it handled."

"What are you doing?" I asked, as he tugged off his shirt and tossed it aside, revealing a chest rippling with muscles that were impossible not to stare at.

"Just watch and see." With those words Jasin walked confidently across the deck and gave me a wink, his auburn hair shining under the sun. He grabbed onto the ship's rigging and hauled himself up it with his strong arms, making my heart jump into my throat. With a mixture of fear and curiosity I watched his powerful body climb the

6

ropes, going higher and higher, until he reached the top of the mast.

He spread his arms wide to the sun—and then he jumped.

I let out a cry as he fell toward the water, but then his body began to shift and grow. Blood red scales slithered across his skin, forming large wings and a long, snaking tail. Talons sprouted from his hands and fangs appeared from his mouth, and soon there was nothing left of my infuriatingly brave soldier except a formidable dragon in his place.

He flapped his great wings to keep from hitting the water, casting a gust of wind at the ship that sent us reeling. I gripped the railing tight as I watched him fly for the first time, while the other guys moved beside me, their eyes wide. Even Reven, though he crossed his arms like he wasn't impressed.

Jasin flew higher and unleashed a loud roar as he faced us, no doubt showing off because he knew he had an audience. Then he let out a strange sound that I thought might be a laugh before doing a flip in the air, clearly reveling in his new form. Under the sun his crimson scales gleamed, and my fear gave way to amazement. One day we would all be able to change forms like that and fly across the sky— including me. And once we mastered our powers and our new Dragon forms, maybe we'd be able to save the world. Assuming we could learn to work together first.

"He's going to be more insufferable than ever now," Reven said.

"No doubt," Slade agreed.

"I can fix that." With a wave of his hand, Auric sent a strong gust of wind flying toward Jasin, right as he did another flip. I arched an eyebrow at Auric, but he just shrugged.

Jasin awkwardly flapped his leathery wings to steady himself, but he couldn't regain his balance and began spiraling out of control. His scales rippled and shifted as if he was becoming human again while he plummeted from the sky. I gasped as his large reptilian body hit the water with a loud smack, sending waves across the deck and drenching the four of us. He sank below the water and I nearly reached for Reven to beg him to save Jasin, but then an auburn head surfaced in front of us.

Jasin tossed his wet hair back and grinned. "Is that the best you've got?"

Yeah, we had a lot of work ahead of us.

2

KIRA

J asin practiced flying for another few hours while Reven and Auric guided our boat with waves and wind. Slade disappeared below deck, claiming all that open sky bothered him. He'd always been distant, but I sensed after my night with Jasin it had only gotten worse. He'd also been hit with a bad case of seasickness, which probably wasn't helping matters.

The area below deck was cramped and dark, almost like a cave, which was probably why Slade preferred it. This ship had been given to us by Calla, the High Priestess of the Fire God, and her four mates. It wasn't very large, just big enough for a small crew to maneuver, and I imagined it had once been used by them for fishing or for travel when needed.

I hoped Calla and her men were still safe. After we'd

fought off the Onyx Army soldiers and escaped the Fire Temple, we'd spotted Sark, the Crimson Dragon, flying over it. Would he hurt Calla or her priests to get information out of us, even though they all served the Fire God too? I wasn't sure, but from here on out we had to assume that the Dragons knew about us. We could no longer hide in the shadows and hope that would protect us. Soon we would have to face them.

As night fell, my mates and I converged on the deck to eat supper together. We'd left most of our gear and supplies behind with our horses in the Fire Realm, which would soon prove to be a problem. Calla and her men had been thoughtful enough to stock the ship with food and other necessities, but that would only last us a short time. Once we reached the Air Realm we'd have to get more supplies and find another way to travel.

I broke off a piece of bread and passed it to Jasin, who did the same before passing it to Slade. "How many days will it take us to reach the Air Realm?" I asked.

"It depends where we're planning to dock," Auric said, as he took the bread from Slade. "We're making good time though."

"What are the options?" Slade asked.

Auric cocked his head as he considered. "There's the capital city, Stormhaven. It's the closest to the Air Temple, although we'll still have to travel on land for another week to get there. From a logistics perspective it's the clear choice, since we can reach it in three days and will be able to obtain new horses and supplies there." He drew in a long breath, his face grim. "The problem is that my family's palace is in Stormhaven."

"And the other option?" Reven asked.

"We continue past Stormhaven and around the bend for another five days to Galeport, then backtrack on land to the Air Temple."

"How much longer will that add?" Slade asked.

"Almost three weeks."

"Three weeks?" I asked, with a sigh. "I don't think we can spare that long. Not when the Dragons might already be hunting for us."

"If so, they'll eventually head to the temples to try to stop us," Jasin said. "The faster we get to them, the better."

"No, the less time we're on this ship the better," Slade grumbled, pushing his food away while clutching his stomach.

"We could disguise Auric and slip him into the city unnoticed," Reven suggested. I suspected he had plenty of experience doing that sort of thing from his former career as an assassin.

"Stormhaven it is," I said. "We'll sneak into the city, get what we need, and leave as soon as we can for the Air Temple."

Auric nodded. "I'll make the adjustments to our course with Reven."

It was the right decision, but I was disappointed I wouldn't be meeting Auric's family, even if that was probably for the best. Auric was a prince who had grown up in a life of luxury. I was a commoner who'd once made a living as a huntress, a bandit, and a traveling merchant. We weren't exactly suitable for each other, and even though Auric claimed he didn't care about our difference in status, his family certainly would. And then there was the whole Dragon thing we had to keep a secret too.

"Now that that's settled, tell us what happened the other night," Auric said. "You told us about the Fire God and what he said, but you didn't talk much about the actual bonding."

Jasin arched an eyebrow. "What, you want all the naughty details?"

"No, of course not," Auric replied quickly. "I simply want to know what to expect. Did anything...unusual happen?"

I glanced over at Jasin. "You *did* set me on fire."

"What?" Reven asked, his head snapping up.

Jasin grinned. "Yes, when we uh...completed. I assume that was the bond taking hold and passing my powers to her."

"Kira," Slade said, in that low, rumbling voice I would never grow tired of hearing. "Are you in any pain?"

"No, why?"

Slade rubbed the back of his neck without meeting my eyes. "A woman's first time can be...difficult."

"Oh." My cheeks flushed. "I'm all right. And if there was any pain, my healing powers must have taken care of it."

Another benefit of being the representative of the Spirit Goddess.

Slade nodded and blew out a breath. "Good."

"You know I would never hurt Kira," Jasin said, looking offended at even the suggestion. "Trust me, I took good care of her. *Multiple* times."

Reven rolled his eyes. "Yes, we've heard all about your sexual prowess."

Gods, could this moment be any more awkward? My skin felt like it was on fire all over again. I coughed. "Jasin made the experience very...pleasant."

Jasin leaned back against the railing with a cocky grin. "I tried. Everyone should have a good first time, don't you all think?"

Slade let out a soft grunt. "Good? Mine was fast and awkward."

"Oh yeah?" Jasin asked. "Tell us about it. Who was the lucky lady?"

Slade's frown deepened as he glanced at me. "I'm not sure this is an appropriate conversation for us to have."

"It's fine," I said, waving it away. "I know you all had other women before you met me. I'm interested in learning everything about your pasts. Or whatever you're willing to share with me, anyway."

The men all hesitated and remained silent, but then Jasin spoke up. "Fine, I'll start. My first time was with one of my brother's friends. She was older than me and taught me how to please a woman."

"How much older?" Slade asked, arching an eyebrow.

"Only a few years. I think she was secretly interested in my brother, but he preferred men and I was the closest she could get." Jasin shrugged. "Both of us knew it wasn't anything serious, and we made each other happy for a while before she married someone else." He took a sip of water and gestured at Slade with the jug. "But if you're so right-eous, tell us your story."

Slade stared down at the untouched food in front of him. "My first time was with a girl in my village. We grew up together and it seemed natural we would be married one day. Neither one of us knew what we were doing during that first time. But we figured it out together eventually over the years."

"What happened to her?" I asked, unable to stop myself.

His green eyes focused on me. "We never got married, if that's what you're asking."

I had a dozen more questions, but Slade's tone implied he had nothing more to say on the matter. I sighed and turned to Reven. "And you?"

"You don't want to hear my story."

"Well, now we definitely do," Jasin said.

Reven glared at him. "Fine, but it's not all fond memories like your stories." He ripped off chunks of his bread and threw them into the ocean without care. "I had to get by on the streets somehow after my parents were killed, and I discovered people will pay to have sex with young men. Quite handsomely."

Stunned silence met his words. I had no idea his parents had been killed, only that he'd told me he'd gotten his swords from his father, and I never would have guessed he'd spent part of his life doing something like that. There was so much more about his past—and everyone else's—that I wanted to uncover. But I had a feeling Reven's would be the darkest...and the hardest to crack.

"I'm sorry," I said, brushing my hand against his, where it rested on the deck.

He yanked his hand away. "Don't be. I'll do whatever it takes to survive. You should know that by now."

"On that cheerful note, what about you, Auric?" Jasin asked.

Auric had been silent the entire conversation, and now he brushed crumbs off his lap. "That's not something I wish to discuss with the group."

Reven arched an eyebrow. "It can't be any worse than my story."

"Maybe he's still waiting for his first time," Jasin teased, and Reven snickered in response.

Slade shook his head. "Leave him alone."

"I'm only trying to get to know my companions better," Jasin said, spreading his hands wide. "If we're going to be stuck together for the rest of our lives and sharing the same woman, we need to be able to talk about these things."

Auric stood and cast a sharp glance at Jasin. "You may be comfortable discussing these matters with everyone, but I am not. And I'd prefer if you respected my privacy in this matter."

He walked away and slipped below deck, while Jasin called out, "Auric, wait! I didn't mean anything by it!"

I shot Jasin a harsh look before going after Auric, while Slade just shook his head again. Every time I thought the five of us might be getting closer, something like this happened. I was beginning to think sharing four strong-willed men was never going to work out.

3

AURIC

I raked a hand through my blond hair, which had grown longer than I preferred over the last few days, while emotion churned inside me. I shouldn't have reacted that way—now they'd all suspect there was a reason for my vehement response. Perhaps I should have made up a story to placate them, but I couldn't lie to Kira. And she'd have to learn the truth eventually.

Kira came through the hatch and joined me below deck, her lovely face showing concern and her red hair a little wild from the wind. "I'm sorry about all that. Please ignore Jasin. He's simply trying to get a rise out of you. You know how he is."

I turned toward her and frowned at the worry in her eyes. Perhaps the time for truth was now. "I know. The problem is...he's right."

"What do you mean?"

I drew in a deep breath. "I've never been with a woman before."

She blinked. "You haven't?"

I rested my hands on her upper arms and gazed into her entrancing hazel eyes. "I'm sorry I didn't tell you sooner. I was waiting for the right moment, but it's hard for me to admit that I am lacking the knowledge or skills I require. Especially in something I wish to become an expert at."

"You don't need to be ashamed. Until the other night, I was inexperienced as well."

"Yes, it's probably fortunate that Jasin was the first one and not me, even if it made me jealous knowing he was claiming you."

She slid her arms around my neck and pressed a soft kiss to my jaw. "Don't be jealous. Soon we'll reach the Air Temple and then we will be bonded too. We can become experienced together."

"It's not as simple as that," I said, shaking my head. "A man is easy to please, but a woman...a woman takes skill and practice to satisfy. At least, that's what I've learned from the books I've read on the subject."

Her lips quirked up in an amused smile. "Books?"

"The library in Stormhaven has a selection of books dedicated to bedroom skills. I've studied them all, so I know the theories and such, but I suspect it will be a different matter entirely to put what I read about into practice."

"Oh, Auric." She laughed softly and then pulled my mouth down to hers. Her lips were sweet, but as her tongue slid against mine I took control of the kiss, taking it deeper. I may have been inexperienced in bed, but kissing? *That* I was an expert on.

Kira's hands slipped under my shirt as I tugged at her lower lip with my teeth. While her palms smoothed across my chest, I trailed kisses down her neck, finding the spots that made her sigh. If nothing else, I was a fast learner—and I was going to make Kira my new object of study. I would explore her own body until I knew it better than my own. I would uncover every way to make her cry out my name in pleasure.

But there was more I had to tell her first.

I caught her face in my hands and met her eyes. "Kira, there's something else too."

"What is it?" she asked.

Before I could speak, Jasin dropped down into the cabin, interrupting me. I didn't pull away from Kira. Let him see that she was mine too. Though if he was bothered by it, he didn't show it.

"Sorry about all of that earlier," Jasin said, surprising me with his sincerity. Jasin and I had never gotten along, but perhaps he was making an effort now that it was clear we were both going to be a part of each other's lives for good, especially since we both loved Kira. Which gave me an idea.

"I didn't mean anything by what I said, and I should have let it go," Jasin continued. "You don't owe the rest of us anything, especially me. If you want to keep part of your past a secret, that's none of my business."

"Thank you for the apology." I hesitated, considering my next move. "But perhaps you can help me with something."

His eyebrows darted up. "Help you? How?"

"I need you to teach me the art of pleasing a woman."

Jasin burst into laughter. "Oh Gods, that's hilarious." He laughed again, but then noticed Kira and I were not in on the joke. His smile dropped into a frown. "Wait, you're serious. Oh. Wow. So you truly are inexperienced. Damn."

"I am, yes. You were correct. I've never had a first time." I gave Kira a heated glance. "Not yet."

"But...how?" Jasin asked. "You're a good-looking guy and a prince too. I can't imagine you couldn't find a woman or three to take to bed."

"It's tradition in the Air Realm for the nobility to remain virgins until marriage, both men and women. I've had plenty of opportunities, but I wanted to wait until I found my forever mate."

"I'm honored," Kira said, giving me a warm smile.

Jasin raked a hand through his already messy hair. "But why me? You and I barely get along as it is. I doubt getting naked together will help."

"It has to be you," I said. "You're the most experienced of us all and you've already bonded with Kira. Besides, we both know Slade and Reven would never agree."

"True." His gaze shifted to Kira. "Are you okay with this?"

She considered us both, her eyes dancing with interest. "The Fire God did say you needed to learn to work together..."

"Somehow I doubt this is what he meant," Jasin muttered.

"Jasin, despite our differences, we both want Kira to be happy," I said. "Though I realize this will be awkward at first, eventually all four of us are going to be sharing her. Maybe at the same time, if that's something she wants."

"Is it?" Jasin asked her.

Her cheeks flushed with obvious desire. "I think so."

Oh yes, she definitely liked the idea of us sharing her at once. The thought aroused me as well, but such a thing was fairly common in the Air Realm. My older sister had two husbands, and both my parents openly shared their beds with others on the side. I was more surprised that Jasin, from the uptight Fire Realm, was even considering this plan.

But he seemed satisfied by Kira's answer. "All right, I'll do it."

I gave him a respectful nod. "Thank you. I promise I'm a quick study."

"Then let's get started." He grabbed his shirt and yanked it off, then tossed it aside.

"Now?" I asked, shocked by his boldness.

Jasin shrugged with a wry grin. "Why wait?"

"Are you sure we're all ready for this?" Kira asked, even though her eyes were roaming all over Jasin's naked chest like she'd never seen anything better in her life.

Jasin stepped close to her. "We won't do anything you don't want to do."

Following his lead, I tugged my shirt over my head and was satisfied by the way Kira's gaze began to devour me too. She ran her tongue along her lower lip in the most alluring way, and there was no mistaking her arousal.

Jasin snaked an arm around Kira's waist and yanked her against him, then captured her mouth in a hot, passionate kiss. I watched them intently, studying the way she melted against him and how his fingers dug into her hips possessively.

But then she broke away and reached for me, pulling me close. Her lips found mine again and I skimmed my fingers across her nipples, feeling how hard they were through the fabric of her dress. Jasin kissed her neck at the same time, trapping Kira between the two of us.

I began to think this plan to involve Jasin might be one of my best yet.

4

KIRA

Last night I'd been a virgin. Now I was pressed between two gorgeous men, their hands and lips lavishing attention on my body. Jasin kissed my neck, while Auric claimed my mouth. Two hands stroked my breasts, and two others cupped my behind and gave it a quick squeeze. All I could do was relax into their touch and succumb to the overwhelming lust they stirred inside me.

I reached for them too, sliding my hands across their hard chests. Jasin was more muscular, a fighter through and through, while Auric was taller and leaner, but still strong. Both of them were perfect for me in different ways.

Jasin dragged my dress up over my head, revealing my naked flesh to Auric for the first time. Auric gazed down at me with a mix of reverence and hunger, taking me all in like he was memorizing every inch.

"Turn around," he said. "I want to see all of you."

I slowly spun, trying not to feel self-conscious under the gaze of both men. My natural inclination was to cover my breasts or my mound, but I kept my arms at my side, channeling a little of the bravery Jasin had taught me. These were my mates, and if I couldn't be naked with them, then who?

"Beautiful," Auric said, his voice rough. "The Gods could not have made you any better."

I flushed as I turned back to him, warm from his compliments. "I want to see you too."

"Whatever you desire." He reached for his trousers and my pulse quickened, but then we heard a sound above us that made us freeze.

Slade dropped below deck, his movements rushed. "We have a—"

He stopped when he saw I was standing completely naked before the other two men. The urge to cover myself or turn away became almost unbearable, but he was going to see me naked eventually—and I wanted to see his reaction.

He quickly looked away, as if shielding his eyes from the sight of my bare skin. "I'm sorry. I didn't know the three of you were...together like this."

"It's all right," I said, trying to hide my disappointment at his response. "Is something wrong?"

"Water elementals are surrounding the ship. Reven tried to speed us past them, but they're turning the sea to ice around us."

Jasin swore under his breath as he charged forward, still wearing nothing but his trousers. "I can fix that."

"Be careful," I said, as I quickly grabbed my dress and pulled it back on. "Remember, the ship is all wood."

We scrambled up the ladder and onto the deck, where Reven glowered at the sea. Our ship was marooned in a large patch of ice in the middle of the ocean, though I didn't see any elementals yet.

"About time," Reven snapped at us. "I've been turning the ice back to water, but there are too many of them down there."

"I've got this." Jasin leaped onto the railing and into the air, shifting into a dragon before he hit the ice. His change was faster this time, and he flapped his wings and blasted the ice with fire from his great fanged mouth.

"They won't last long against his fire magic," Auric said.

Slade watched Jasin fly higher with a frown. "No, but there are a lot more of them than him."

"And that's if he doesn't set the entire ship on fire and kill us for them," Reven muttered.

As Jasin took out the ice in front of us, the elementals burst onto the back of the ship with a crash of waves that sent cold seawater across our feet. At first I could only stare at the large, swirling masses of water with arms, glowing yellow eyes, and huge gaping mouths. But as Auric shot a gust of wind to knock the elementals back and Slade pulverized them with small pieces of metal, I shook myself out of the fear and shock.

I quickly formed a ball of flame in my hand, but then hesitated, worried I might miss and do damage to the ship. I hadn't had much chance to practice my magic yet, and we'd decided it was safer for Jasin to train me once we were on land again. But this was the only way I could stop the elementals—they were immune to normal weapons.

"I'll cover you," Reven said. "My magic doesn't work on them anyway."

I nodded. Auric and Slade had knocked two elementals back into the water, but I suspected that wouldn't stop them for long. Meanwhile, Jasin was fighting a large group at the front of the ship, his wings flapping as he did passes over them to rain down fire. I wasn't sure how long he could keep that up though, especially since his dragon form was still so new to him.

Three elementals glided across the deck toward us and began shooting strong bursts of icy water as us. Reven reached out and diverted the water back into the ocean before it could hit us, but the elementals kept getting closer.

"Dragons...must...die..." one of them said, surprising me. I'd never realized they could speak in our language.

"We're not like the other Dragons!" I called out, though it was clear there would be no reasoning with them.

The elementals suddenly charged us, their liquid bodies slicing through the wooden deck of the ship and sending splinters flying. One knocked Auric off the ship and into the water, while another began wrestling with Slade. The third came for me.

I threw my ball of flame, but only managed to graze the thing's shoulder, where the fire sizzled out. So much for that plan. Reven shot water at the elemental to protect me, but all it did was join the creature's body, making it stronger.

The elemental wrapped a cold, watery hand around my neck and lifted me up into the air. I forced fire to burst from my palms as I grabbed onto his head, which made the monster let out something like a scream. I kept up the pressure, making the flames hotter and stronger, and the elemental began to dissipate in front of my eyes. When it let me go I tumbled back into Reven, who steadied me while the elemental turned to steam and vanished.

I rubbed my aching throat, my heart racing, but there was no time to stop and recover. Slade was still grappling with the other elemental, using sharp pieces of the broken deck to attack it from all sides. I'd never seen him use wood before, only stone and metal, but there was little of that available on the ship and he must have had to improvise.

Auric burst out of the water, floating high into the air as if he was flying, and relief shot through me. He blasted an elemental across the deck and into the ocean, while Slade slammed the other one down against the deck. I rushed forward and used fire on it to take it out, while Jasin seared the ones in the sea. Slowly the elementals dipped back under the waves, retreating from the battle.

When they vanished, Jasin plummeted from the sky and collapsed on the deck in human form, the momentum ripping another hole into the wood as he rolled to a stop.

"Jasin!" I called out as I rushed over to him, worried he was injured from the fall or the battle. I reached his side and turned him over, but he only gave me a weary smile.

"It's nice to know I'm still your favorite."

"Hardly." I wasn't sure whether to smack him upside the

head or kiss him senseless, which was pretty normal with Jasin. Instead I sat back on the deck beside him, exhausted after using my magic. No wonder the men trained every day to build their control and their fortitude. If I was ever going to get better with fire, I'd need a lot more practice.

Slade kneeled beside me and rested a hand on my shoulder. "Are you all right?"

I nodded and leaned into his strong touch while gazing across the ship. Our deck was a mess, the wood torn up and splintered, with a few gaping holes in it. There was so much water on the deck, and I couldn't tell if it was from the elementals or if the ship was taking it on. "I'm fine, but our ship isn't."

"I might be able to fix that," Slade said, his stony eyes surveying the deck.

"We have a bigger problem," Auric suddenly called out, drawing our attention.

Off the starboard side of the boat a massive wave was forming, created by the remaining water elementals. It was easily as tall as the ship. And it was coming right for us.

5
KIRA

I gaped at the giant wave speeding across the ocean, which would engulf our ship in only minutes. "What do we do?"

Jasin hefted himself up to a sitting position with a groan. "I'll have to face them again."

"You can't." I grabbed his arm to hold him back. If he couldn't even stand, how was he supposed to deal with the elementals?

He shrugged me off. "What other option is there?"

"We run," Reven said.

Auric began filling the sails with air to speed us away, while Reven controlled the water currents around the ship. Slade assisted by tying ropes or adjusting the sails, while I tried to give Jasin some of my strength with the touch of my hands. It didn't seem to do much, maybe because I'd worn myself out already too.

And the giant wave kept coming closer.

"We can't outrun it," Auric called out after a few minutes, the wind whipping at his golden hair. "We have to brace for impact!"

"Get below deck," Slade told me and Jasin in a firm tone.

"Not a chance." Jasin forced himself to his feet, leaning heavily against the mast.

"Then protect Kira. She's the most important thing on this ship."

Slade's overprotectiveness sometimes got on my nerves, but I didn't have time to argue that I could take care of myself. Not when the massive wave would hit us in mere moments. "We need to work together," I said. "That's the only way through this."

Reven faced the approaching water with his head high. "I'll hold back the water as best I can."

"I can try to put a bubble of air around us," Auric said.

Slade rubbed his beard as he considered. "I'll reinforce the ship. Make it stronger so it won't break apart under the wave."

"Kira and I will blast those elementals," Jasin said.

It wasn't a perfect plan and we'd likely all be sent to the bottom of the ocean, but it was something. It gave me strength knowing that even if my mates squabbled in their free time, they came together when it counted.

"Here it comes!" Reven yelled, as he braced himself against the railing. He cast a determined look at the wave and held it back as it came toward us, but all he could do was slow it down. If he'd had his dragon form maybe he could stop it, but there were too many elementals controlling this water.

The enormous wave crested over the ship, raining saltwater down on us and blocking out the sky. Fear gripped my throat as Auric raised his arms, causing the water to slam against an invisible wall around us. Slade bent down and rested his palms on the wood and metal of the deck, while the ship begin to creak and groan.

The wave drenched the entire ship with a great crash and sent it careening to the side, but Auric and Reven's magic kept us dry. Water buffeted their defenses relentlessly, and the two men were forced back while our small bubble of safety shrank.

From the view around us, we might as well have been completely underwater. Maybe we were, with the way the ship was lurching, making it hard for us to stand. I lost my footing and crashed into Slade, but he caught me and held me against him, as if he could protect me with his sheer size and willpower.

The wave didn't seem to end and I could tell my mates were losing the battle, as was the ship, which splintered apart under the pressure from the water. But then the elementals appeared through the wave, their glowing eyes giving them away.

I gripped Jasin's arm. "We have to stop them!"

He nodded, his face weary but his will unwavering. Together we stepped in front of the other men and sought out the elementals, but there were too many of them and my magic was still untrained. We couldn't afford for me to miss. No, we needed Jasin's magic.

I took Jasin's hand and felt the bond between us flare bright. I closed my eyes and willed my energy and healing magic from the Spirit Goddess to flow into him. As it did, a wave of exhaustion swept through me, even as Jasin's body began to glow faintly. I had no idea if this would work or how long I could do this, but we needed Jasin more than we needed me right now. He was the only one who could save us.

Jasin conjured fire in his other hand and it burned so hot it was almost blue. He cast it at the elemental nearest us and it went up in a wisp of steam immediately. He lobbed another ball of flame at the next one, and the next, clutching my other hand tight the entire time. The never-ending downpour buffering the ship began to ease slightly. And as he worked I felt his resolve, his fear, his courage, and his exhilaration through the bond as if they were my own emotions.

The last elemental went up in a spray of mist, and the wave suddenly ceased its attack, dropping back into the ocean. The ship rolled violently and the deck was splintered and cracked in numerous places, but was otherwise intact. All four of my mates were alive, although exhausted and drenched with saltwater.

We did it.

That was my last thought before fatigue swept through me and I collapsed onto the deck, still clutching Jasin's hand.

6

SLADE

Kira's body hit the deck and I rushed toward her, even though Jasin was already kneeling over her. I knocked him out of the way and lifted Kira's small form into my arms. Her body was completely limp and her head rolled against my shoulder, her eyes closed, but she was alive at least. *Kira, what did he do to you?*

"I can take her," Jasin said, reaching for Kira again.

I pinned him with a stern gaze. "You've done enough."

"Is she all right?" Auric asked, his face lined with worry.

"She's still breathing," Reven said.

"She needs rest." I began to make my way toward the hatch leading below deck. The other guys followed right at my heels, while Kira's head rested snugly against my chest. I'd already been terrified for her during the elemental attack, but seeing her collapse had been too much and I'd been forced to jump into action. She seemed so small and fragile in my arms, even though I knew she was as fierce as any of us. If I could keep her cradled in my arms and safe forever, I would. She would hate it, but I wouldn't care if it meant no harm would ever befall her.

Gods, when had I begun to care so much for her? There was no denying it. I was fond of her, though I was hesitant to admit it even to myself. It had to be that damn mate bond between us making me want to protect her and be near her at all times. And it would only get worse once we were truly bonded at the Earth Temple.

As I jumped down into the lower quarters with Kira nestled in my arms, water splashed everywhere. It was up to my knees thanks to the wave that had attacked us, but otherwise the ship appeared intact down here. I'd have to do a more thorough appraisal soon, but first I had to get Kira settled.

Auric righted a hammock and I gently placed Kira into it, then brushed hair off her face with my knuckles. She didn't even stir, and I stared at her chest for some time to confirm she was truly breathing.

Then I turned toward Jasin and slammed him back against the nearest wall. "What did you do to her?"

His eyes widened. "Me? I did nothing!"

My grip tightened around his shirt. "Then what happened to her?"

"She took my hand and gave me her power. Our bond went berserk or something. I don't know!"

"That's why you were glowing," Auric said from behind me.

I released Jasin with a low growl, and he straightened up and glared at me in return. "I swear, I didn't do anything," he said. "I was completely wiped out, but then she touched me and I suddenly had a ton of energy again and I could summon more fire than ever." His face softened as he looked over at Kira. "I had no idea it would do this to her."

"She probably didn't know either," Auric said.

Reven shrugged. "She did this to herself. It's not Jasin's fault."

I swung my angry stare over to him. "No one asked for your opinion, deserter."

Reven's eyes narrowed at me and my fists clenched in return. Normally I was the calm, clear-headed one of the group who could ignore their constant bickering, but not when Kira was suffering like this. Jasin was the cause this time, but Reven had abandoned Kira before when she needed him most. She'd forgiven him somehow, but if it were up to me we'd be looking for a new man to represent water.

Auric touched Kira's forehead with the back of his hand. "She's going to be okay. She just needs rest."

I stiffened. "We don't know that. She's never been like this before."

"I'm worried too," Jasin said. "But I can feel her through our bond and she's still there. I think she'll be fine after she gets some sleep. The best thing we can do for her is to get this ship moving again."

I drew in a long breath and allowed my muscles to relax. "All right, but one of us needs to keep watch over her at all times in case something changes. And I'm taking first watch."

"No, we need you to fix the ship," Jasin said, which made me only want to slam him against the wall again. If he thought he was going to step up and be the leader of this group he was going to be met with some resistance, even if he'd bonded with Kira first.

"He's right," Auric said. "Reven and I can't get the ship moving again without your repairs in place, and Jasin's magic can't do much in that regard."

Jasin nodded. "I'll take first watch."

"I'll get the next one," Reven said, crossing his arms. "Once I get the water off this ship, you won't need me for a while."

I pressed my palm to my forehead, fighting off a rising headache, no doubt from dealing with Kira's annoying mates. "Fine."

I climbed up the ladder with heavy steps, my own exhaustion taking hold of me now that the thrill of the battle and the fear over Kira's collapse was behind me. I'd continue to worry about her until she was awake and could tell me herself she was okay, but there were other ways to protect her too. Like repairing this ship.

As the ship swelled and rolled, another wave of seasickness reminded me I should have stayed on land from the beginning. Without firm ground under my feet I was mostly useless in a battle, although I'd discovered I could control wood as long as all the life had left it. Living things were the domain of the Spirit Goddess, but old, hard wood was as lifeless as stone and seemed to fall under my control.

I used that power now to mend the splintered mast so that Auric could get the ship sailing again soon and allow us to continue on to the Air Temple. And after that...the Earth Temple, where I would fully bond with Kira. At first, I'd resisted the idea. Then I'd come to terms with it and considered it my duty. Now I was anxious to get there sooner than later. Once I was a Dragon I would be able to defend Kira and the others better. Gods knew Jasin needed all the help he could get in that area.

But the act of bonding would be a problem. Even if I desired Kira physically, things between us could never go beyond friendship and duty. I would never love a woman again without reservation, and even if I could, I wasn't comfortable with the idea of sharing her with other men. There was no way Kira could love all of us equally in the end, and I wasn't willing to be someone's second—or third or fourth—choice. I'd already been left for another man once. I was never opening myself up to that kind of pain again.

7

KIRA

W hen I opened my eyes I found Reven in the hammock beside me, wearing nothing but his trousers. His cool skin pressed against mine, and I discovered I wore only my threadbare chemise as well. One of my mates must have changed me out of my soaked dress at some point.

With Reven's eyes closed he looked peaceful for once, especially with his black hair messy. Younger, too. Or perhaps he appeared his true age for once. How he would look if he didn't have his dark past weighing on him all the time.

The second I moved, his eyes snapped open and fixed on me. They were the color of the waves around the ship and just as cold.

"What are you doing here?" I asked, as I slowly rolled

toward him, the hammock drawing us close together. "And without a shirt on?"

"We thought touching you might heal you faster. Like when you heal us." His jaw clenched, but he didn't move away. "It was Auric's idea."

"Of course it was." I rested my hands on the muscular ridges of his chest. For healing, naturally. "How long have I been out?"

"Almost two days."

"Two *days*?" I pushed on his chest to rise to a sitting position. "What happened to me?"

He sat up next to me and shrugged. "You collapsed after we fought off the water elementals. We brought you in here to rest."

I scrubbed a hand over my face as the memories came back. "I gave Jasin my energy and strength so he could fight the elementals off, but I must have drained myself in the process."

"Seems that way."

I'd have to be more careful in the future, especially if it knocked me out for so long. I practically fell out of the hammock and righted myself on shaky legs, while my stomach ached with a hollow feeling and my vision blurred. "Oh Gods, I'm starving."

"I'm sure we can find you something." Reven got to his feet in one smooth motion that made me look like a graceless animal. He grabbed his shirt and tossed it on, the muscles in his back flexing and commanding my attention. It was truly unfair for someone so difficult to be so irresistible.

With Reven right behind me, I slowly climbed up the ladder and moved through the hatch onto the main deck, squinting against the bright sun. Where I'd expected disaster and wreckage, all I saw was the ship looking almost as good as new. Gods, I really had been out a long time.

"Kira!" Jasin called out from above me. "You're awake!"

He slid down a rope from the main mast and landed at my feet, while Auric floated down until his boots lightly touched the deck. Slade hopped down from the upper deck as he approached us. Yes, everyone on this ship was more graceful than me today.

Auric touched my face softly. "It's good to see you up again."

"You've learned a new trick," I said, leaning into his palm.

"Yes, and it's definitely coming in handy. Not all of us are eager to climb the ropes like Jasin here."

Slade gripped my shoulders and spun me around to take me in. "Kira, are you well?"

"I'm okay, thanks. Just hungry." I tried to pat down my hair, which was more unruly than ever, not helped by the warm breeze out here. "I can't believe I slept so long."

"Let me get you something to eat," Jasin said, before darting off.

"He feels responsible for what happened to you," Auric said quietly.

"He *is* responsible," Slade growled.

I reached for the railing to steady myself, feeling a bit

lightheaded. "No, it was all my own doing. Don't blame Jasin for this."

"What don't you sit down?" Auric said, taking my elbow and leading me along the ship. He helped me onto a nearby barrel, while the other men hovered around me. They'd already been over-protective of me, and now that I'd passed out in front of them I'd never get a moment to myself again.

"I'm fine, really," I said, though I did feel better now that I was sitting.

Reven handed me a flask, scowling the entire time. "Drink this."

I sighed at him, but then took a long sip of cool, deliciously fresh water. Before I knew it the flask was empty and my head had stopped spinning quite so much. With a flick of his fingers, Reven summoned more water into the flask, while Jasin returned with a spread of food—bread, cheese, and some fried fish. Enough to feed all of us, but he set it in front of me alone.

"Thank you, this is perfect," I said, as I popped a piece of cheese into my mouth.

"Reven caught us all some fish earlier, and I fried them up while Auric and Slade fixed the ship," Jasin said with a grin. Through our bond I felt him near me and sensed his emotions—mainly relief, with a touch of guilt and worry.

I managed a small smile at the group of men. "It's nice to see you all working together."

"Don't get used to it." Reven crossed his arms, but that only made me smile wider.

"Can you tell us what happened the other day?" Auric asked.

I took another sip of water before continuing. "I could tell Jasin was exhausted and I still don't know how to control fire very well, so I tried to lend him my energy and strength."

"It definitely worked. I'd never felt so powerful before." Jasin stroked my hair tenderly while I ate. "I only wish it hadn't drained you in the process."

"I'll have to be careful in the future. I'm still learning how to use all this magic and I haven't even begun my fire training." The thought of everything I had ahead of me was daunting. I'd have to master all five elements, and quickly. Along with everything else that came with being the Black Dragon.

"You just need to practice," Slade said. "It's the same as learning any new skill. The more you do it the better you'll get at it, and the longer you'll be able to keep it going."

I nodded. Archery had been the same way at first. When I'd first joined the bandits I had never held a bow before and thought I would never be good at it. Now the only one who could rival me with a bow was Jasin.

"We're growing stronger every day," Auric said. "Imagine how powerful we'll be once we're all bonded to you."

"Imagine how powerful the other Dragons are now," Reven countered. "They've had centuries to practice their magic."

"Let's hope we won't encounter one anytime soon." I

couldn't help but glance back the way we'd come, wondering if Sark's blood-red wings were trailing behind us. Sooner or later we would have to face the Dragons—and we definitely weren't ready for them yet.

8

JASIN

That night I sought out Kira below deck after giving her a bit more time to recover. As I stepped down the ladder, she was staring at Auric's map of the four Realms, her finger resting near the Air Temple and her brow creased in thought. Her red hair hung loose around her shoulders, framing her graceful neck and that beautiful face I could stare at forever. *Mine*, something inside me whispered with satisfaction.

Though I knew she'd bond with the other men soon, I took great pride in being her first mate. She'd been hesitant to trust me at first, between my past as a ladies' man and a soldier in the Onyx Army, but eventually I'd won her over and proven my devotion to her. And a good thing too, because I'd realized before we even reached the Fire Temple that I was in love with her. I'd never felt so strongly about any woman before, and now I couldn't imagine a life without Kira in it.

"How are you feeling?" I asked, when she glanced up at me.

"Better, thanks." She pushed the map aside as I moved behind her and began massaging her shoulders. With a soft sigh she tilted her head back, relaxing under my firm hands. "That feels nice."

"Good." I brushed aside her hair and slid her dress down her shoulders so I could better knead her soft skin. "When you collapsed in front of us I was so worried. The other guys were too. Don't do that again, okay?"

"I'll try not to, but I can't make any guarantees. I'm still testing the limits of these new powers and I have a lot to learn. "

"Just be careful. I've never seen Slade so upset before."

She turned her head toward me. "Slade was upset?"

"Very. All of us were. Even Reven." I pressed my thumbs into the spot between her shoulder blades where I could tell she was extra tense. "At least I could still sense you through our bond so I knew you would be okay. The others could only trust my word on that."

"I understand. I can feel you through the bond too." She leaned back into my touch. "I can sense where you are and sometimes feel your emotions."

I chuckled softly. "Not sure I'm thrilled with *that* aspect of the bond."

"Why, are you hiding something from me?" she asked in a teasing voice.

"Not at all. Just as long as you can't read my thoughts. Although if you could, you'd see all the things I'd like to do to you now that we're finally alone."

"No mind reading, I promise." She stood and turned toward me with a seductive grin. "But maybe you can show me some of these things..."

"Are you sure? You're still recovering."

"I'm all right. Besides, we can test out the theory that touching gives me energy in return." But as soon as she stepped into my eager arms, she swayed a little and I found myself supporting her weight. She pressed a hand to her forehead. "Sorry, I got a little lightheaded there."

I held her tight against me as concern overcame my desire. "How about we just relax together instead?"

She nodded. "Probably a good idea. I'm sorry though."

I pressed a kiss to her lips. "Don't be sorry. All I want is to be by your side."

"Thanks. I wish I had the strength to do more. I'd like to continue what we started in the Fire Temple."

"Soon. Once we're on dry land again maybe."

Together we climbed into the hammock and she curled up in my arms. A sense of satisfaction and peace settled over me as she tucked her head against my neck. Before I met Kira I'd been the type of man who had a new woman in every city I visited, and I'd only spent a single night with each of them. Cuddling with a woman was out of the question—that was how people got attached, and that was the last thing I'd wanted. Until Kira.

"Auric will want to join us too," she mused, as she

played with the collar of my shirt idly. "Are you sure you're all right with that?"

"I don't mind. I've shared women with other soldiers before, and if it makes you happy then I'm all for it. Even if Auric isn't my favorite person." I wrapped a strand of her red hair around my finger. "Although he's not my least favorite person anymore either."

"No? Who is?"

"Reven."

She snorted. "I think the other guys would probably agree with you."

"He left us when we needed him most. I'm not sure I'll ever trust him again."

"He came back at least," Kira pointed out.

"He should never have left in the first place." Why was Reven even here, when he didn't seemed to care about Kira at all? He wasn't good enough for her. At least Auric—annoying though he may be—was a prince, and he obviously loved Kira as much as I did. Even Slade, who avoided Kira as much as possible, obviously had feelings for her he wasn't ready to admit yet. But Reven? I couldn't tell what he wanted, and I worried he would only hurt her in the end.

"I have to believe the Gods chose all of you for a reason," Kira said.

As I held her close I stared up at the ceiling, the hammock creaking under us, matching the roll of the ship on the waves. "The Fire God said they chose us to help bring out certain aspects in you." For me it was bravery and passion, but I wasn't sure what the others were supposed to be helping Kira with. All Reven brought out in Kira was frustration, and Slade wasn't much better. It would be up to me and Auric to keep her happy during what came ahead, which was why I'd agreed to share her with the prince more than any other reason.

Kira was going to face a number of obstacles in the future and she needed people by her side she could trust, who would support her and help keep her strong no matter what she faced. I'd already pledged my heart, mind, and soul to that task. I had no doubt Auric would too. But would the other two, when the time came?

9

KIRA

As we approached Stormhaven, Auric's wind buffeted our sails and the ship sliced through the waves at an unnatural speed. I stood on the prow and gazed at the capital of the Air Realm in the distance, a barely visible assortment of tall buildings shining bright under the midday sun. With each passing moment it grew in size, and in only a few more hours we'd be stepping onto shore again.

The Air Realm was known as the center of culture in the four Realms, prized for its fine art, music, and literature. Thanks to a rich trade of dyes, spices, and oils, the Air Realm was also the wealthiest kingdom in the world. I'd never been to Stormhaven before in all of my travels, and I couldn't help but feel excited at seeing the City of a Thousand Spires, as it was called.

I wished Tash could be with me, especially since she'd always wanted to visit the Air Realm for the shopping and fine cuisine. She'd been my best friend in Stoneham, where I'd lived the last few years in the Earth Realm, and I missed her greatly. While I enjoyed the presence of my four mates, I missed speaking to a fellow woman now and then. Especially Tash, with her cheerful demeanor and easygoing attitude. Even after I'd killed her abusive father—in self-defense, of course—she'd remained strong and didn't seem to harbor any resentment toward me. I closed my eyes and imagined her now, likely running her family's inn, her dark hair braided as she worked. I prayed to the Gods she was okay and that I would see her again soon.

Auric moved to stand by my side, resting his hands lightly on the railing as he stared across the waves toward the city where he'd been raised. "We'll be there soon."

I turned toward him, examining his handsome, regal face. "Are you nervous?"

"A little. Reven assures me the plan will work, but I can't help but worry I'll be recognized, as it would be difficult to find anyone in Stormhaven who doesn't know my face. If my family finds out I've returned, I'm not sure what will happen. I can't imagine they'll be happy with me after I disappeared without a word when I went to find you."

"They must be worried about you."

"Probably," he said with a sigh. "It would be nice to be see them briefly and let them know I'm safe, but that isn't a good idea."

I hesitated, but then asked the question lingering on my tongue. "Are they loyal to the Black Dragon, like Jasin's family?"

"I'm not sure how to answer that. My parents are good people who want what is best for their kingdom. That means serving the Dragons and bowing to their wishes, but I've also seen my parents stand up to them too. They'll protect the Air Realm however they can."

"I wish some of the other Realms had kings and queens who would think of their people's best interests and stand up to the Dragons sometimes."

"It's not easy. The last ruler who truly stood against the Dragons was the Earth King, and his entire family was slaughtered for it. Except for his youngest daughter, who was only four at the time. The Black Dragon raised the girl as her own daughter to ensure her loyalty, and now the Earth Queen is basically a puppet."

I'd heard that story about the Earth Queen as well. I shuddered. "I can see why no one wants to appear disloyal."

"Exactly. My parents must walk a fine line. So yes, they're loyal to the Dragons. But they're also not." He shrugged. "Politics."

"I don't think I could live that kind of life."

"No, me neither. I was never good at the political maneuverings and courtly intrigue. That life never felt like it was meant for me. I'm much happier now as one of your mates."

"We're lucky to have you. Without your wealth of knowledge, we would be lost. Literally."

"Glad I can be of use." His head tilted as he examined the city again. "I have to admit I'm eager to return to

Stormhaven, even if only for a short while. I've traveled to many places now, but this will always be my home."

"I'm excited to see it. I've heard so much about Stormhaven. The markets. The cafes. The spires."

"Stormhaven gets terrible lightning storms, hence its name," Auric said, as he caught me gazing out at the city with awe. "The spires were originally built to protect the city from lightning strikes, but then it became a trend to build high into the sky to honor the Air God."

"The city is beautiful."

"You have to see it at sunset. There's nothing more stunning than the sun turning the clouds pink and the spires reflecting the light back." He turned toward me and lightly rested his hands on my waist. "I only wish the circumstances of our arrival were different and I could show you around the city and the palace. Maybe even meet my parents."

I swallowed my longing for those very things. "I would like that very much. Someday..."

"Yes, someday." He pressed a quick kiss to my lips before releasing me. "I should probably ease off on the wind and ask Reven to slow the currents as well so that those ships up ahead don't notice we're moving a bit too quickly."

I nodded. "I'll make sure everything is packed up and ready to go."

I headed below deck and found Slade putting the last few things in our bags, including some of the supplies Calla and her priests had provided for us. "Can I do anything to help?"

"No, I think we're ready." He tied off one of the bags and set it with the others.

I moved to the area where I'd kept my things and checked that my bow and sword were ready, along with the small bag I'd brought. "I bet you're excited to be back on land again."

"You have no idea. I can only pray I never have to be out at sea again. I need to be able to see the land at least. If this is my last time on a boat, even better."

I bit my lip and decided not to tell him that much of the Water Realm was made up of tiny islands and the Water Temple was only accessible by boat. By then he would be able to fly at least, although if he hated the ocean I couldn't imagine he'd like the sky much better.

"Did you do much traveling before we met?" I asked.

"No, not at all. I'd only left my village a few times. I never would have imagined I'd get to visit each Realm." Slade rubbed his beard, which had grown longer while we were on the boat. "Then again, I never would have imagined any of this."

"Me neither."

"You've been to the Air Realm before though, haven't you?"

"Yes, a few years ago." I debated revealing more, but that was a story better suited for another day. "Although this is my first visit to Stormhaven."

Reven dropped down onto the lower deck. "Watch your coins. Stormhaven is known for its thieves. All the Air Realm is full of bandits, actually."

I knew that all too well. With any luck, we would never come across the Thunder Chasers, the bandit group I'd once been a part of. At some point I would have to tell my mates about that part of my past, though I worried what they would think of me. Reven probably wouldn't care, but the others? A soldier, a prince, and a blacksmith would not look fondly on the things I'd once done.

"I thought the Air Realm was the wealthiest kingdom," Slade said.

Reven put on his twin swords. "It is. But it also has the weakest guard and the smallest division of the Onyx Army. The people here are peaceful, fat, and happy, with no desire to fight. Which is why thieves run wild here, and why getting in and out of Stormhaven will be easy."

"I hope you're right," I said. "Have you done...jobs here?"

"Two," Reven said. "I poisoned a man who was beating his mistress, on behalf of her sister. I also strangled a woman who was smuggling children on the black market."

A part of me wished I had never asked, and a part of me was fascinated by Reven's cold brutality and how he spoke so matter-of-factly about murder, even if the targets seemed like people who'd deserved it. I'd killed before, numerous times, but only in self-defense. I didn't think I could ever be as casual about taking a life as Reven was. Perhaps that was why the Water God had chosen him—to teach me to do what needed to be done without letting my emotions get in the way.

If so, I had a lot to learn.

10

KIRA

W ithout magic guiding our ship we seemed to creep into the busy harbor, passing boats both bigger and smaller than ours as we approached the dock. Reven shouted out orders to the other men to hoist the sails while he steered the wheel, his dark hair flowing in the wind. With his black clothing and his twin swords at his waist he looked like a pirate captain from the Water Realm. He'd originally claimed to know only a little about sailing, but luckily he'd remembered more than he'd let on. Without his expertise we would have no idea what to do, especially as we brought the ship up to the dock, but he'd clearly spent some time handling a ship before.

Maneuvering a ship like this with five inexperienced people was a challenge, even if the boat wasn't that big. As we neared the dock we came disturbingly close to another larger ship, and it was only with a touch of Reven's magic washing us to the side that we avoided colliding with it.

"Careful!" Jasin called out as he hauled on a rope.

Reven only glared at him as he turned the wheel and eased us up to the dock. Slade dropped the anchor and Jasin leaped out to tie the boat off, while Auric remained below deck, much to his dismay. He was the opposite of Slade and hated being in confined spaces, preferring the open air and the sky around him.

When the ship was secure I took in a breath of fresh air tinged with the smell of fish and something else like faint perfume. We'd made it to Stormhaven, and all around us the port was bustling with activity. Sailors hauled goods on and off boats, men and women in colorful clothing strolled along the marina with umbrellas to block the hot sun, and people at nearby stalls called out to offer food and more. Behind it all, the great city rose up with its many silvery spires glittering under the sun as they reached toward the sky. In the distance, the palace stood on a hill with the tallest spires of all, which disappeared into the clouds.

Jasin drew me in for a hug. "Stay safe."

Our lips brushed and I nodded at him. "We'll be fine."

The plan was for Slade, Reven, and I to go through the city and look for supplies and some new horses, while Jasin and Auric waited on the ship. Jasin had argued he should go with us too, but Reven was the only one beside Auric who had been to the city before, and Slade said he wasn't spending a second longer on the boat. I'd insisted on going too, which meant Jasin had to stay behind to protect the ship with Auric, who needed to stay out of sight until we returned. After night fell we would sneak him out of the city with our new supplies and horses.

"Are we ready?" I asked Slade and Reven.

Reven nodded and hopped off the ship. But as Slade and I followed him onto the dock, a number of soldiers suddenly approached us. They weren't wearing the black scaled armor of the Onyx Army, and instead had smooth metal armor that gleamed gold, with the symbol of the House of Killian etched on their chests. Royal guards.

"Halt," called out the one in the front. He was the only one with a white feathered plume on his helmet, which I assumed meant he was their Captain.

Reven rested a hand on the hilt of his sword, his muscles tense as though he was ready to start slaughtering them all, but I shook my head at him.

I stepped forward with a smile. "Is there a problem, good sirs?"

"All ships that are not registered with the Harbor Master must be searched by order of the King," the Captain said.

I tried to keep my face calm, though my heart was pounding. "Is that truly necessary? As you can see, our ship is small. We don't have anything of interest here. We're simply weary travelers looking for a better life in the Air Realm."

"That may be so, but I have my orders." The Captain glanced between me and the other men, his eyes lingering on Slade's large form for an extra second. "Have you traveled from the Earth Realm?"

He must think that because of Slade's dark skin, which was more common in the Earth Realm. Slade nodded. "Yes, from Mudport."

Jasin drew a bag of coins. "Listen, how about you say you searched the ship and go on your way. We can make it very worth your while."

"Is that so?" the Captain asked, and I held my breath, hoping he'd let us go. Instead he drew his sword and shouted, "Detain these people and search the ship!"

Reven reached for his sword again, but I grabbed his arm to still him. Violence might be his natural instinct for dealing with problems, but these men were only doing their job in service of Auric's family. Perhaps if we used our magic we might be able to escape, but not without drawing a lot of attention from the other people on the docks. Auric would never be able to remain anonymous that way, and word of us might even reach the Dragons. Right now our only advantage was that the Dragons might not know where we were.

"We don't want any trouble." I stepped forward and offered my arms in surrender. My mates grumbled, but they stood down. The Royal Guard dragged us each away from the ship and bound our hands, while their Captain watched. Soon they would begin searching the ship and would find Auric below deck. As rope was tied around my wrists, I tried to think of a way we could cause a distraction to allow Auric to get away unnoticed.

But then Auric emerged and stood above us on the ship's deck. "Let them go," he said. "They're with me."

"Prince Auric?" the Captain asked, before dropping into a hasty bow.

"Yes, it's me. Release my friends." My heart sank as Auric stepped forward, though he didn't look anything like a prince with his longer hair and his worn commoner's clothes. There would be no hiding him now. His family would soon learn he was here, and we would never be able to escape Stormhaven unnoticed.

"I'm sorry, your highness, but I can't do that. In fact, I need you to come with me." The Captain lowered his voice. "Your father has been searching for you and he's ordered us to detain anyone you are found with."

"That's not necessary," Auric said.

The Captain crossed the deck to Auric and spoke quietly. "I know it must have been difficult being kidnapped and held captive all this time, but you don't need to keep up the ruse. You're safe now."

Auric's eyes widened "I'm not being held captive!"

The Captain ignored him and turned toward the rest of his guard, who were also bowing at the prince. "Get those people to the prison! I'll inform the King immediately that his son has been rescued. Now, Prince Auric, if you'll just come with me."

He led Auric to a carriage, and though Auric protested and tried to explain that this was all a misunderstanding, no one seemed to listen. We were hauled into a different carriage forcefully and the door was locked shut, trapping us inside a small, windowless space. I sank back against the threadbare cushions with my hands bound behind my back as our carriage rolled away, leaving Auric behind.

So much for our inconspicuous arrival.

11

REVEN

Two guards shoved me and Kira into a small prison room, before the heavy door closed and locked behind us with a loud slam. I did a quick survey of the room: dark stone walls, a small window with bars, a meager cot with no blankets, one chamber pot in the corner, and rat droppings on the ground. Not the worst prison I'd been thrown into, but not the best either.

After I cut our wrist bindings with a sharp shard of ice, Kira sat on the edge of the cot and buried her face in her hands. "That did not go as planned."

"These things never do, although I wasn't expecting a search of the ship. The Royal Guard has definitely stepped it up since I was last in Stormhaven."

"I hope the others are okay." She ran her fingers through her hair to calm the tangles, her face lined with worry. "Where are Jasin and Slade?"

I inspected the bars on the window, but they were secure. "Being kept in another prison, I assume. Or being questioned."

She sighed heavily. "At least Auric should be safe. They wouldn't hurt him."

"No, but I can't say the same for us."

She glanced at the door, her brow furrowed. "What do we do?"

"We wait and plan our escape."

"Escape? Is that possible?"

I leaned against the heavy door and shrugged. "Wouldn't be the first time I've broken out of a prison like this."

"How?"

"When they come to feed us, we'll fight our way out. They took our weapons, but we still have our magic. Then we'll find Jasin and Slade and get out of here." Along with my swords. I wasn't leaving without them.

She shook her head. "Auric will get us out. We shouldn't use our powers unless we have no other choice."

"We'll see."

We lapsed into silence as I studied the room for any potential weaknesses. I stared out the tiny window, trying to get a sense of where we were, but all I saw were overgrown weeds.

"You did a good job handling the ship today," she said. "Where did you learn to sail?"

There she went again, trying to pry into my past. Why

did she care so much? "Most people in the Water Realm know how to sail a boat. I'm surprised you don't."

"I learned how to paddle small boats, but not a ship of that size, though I did leave the Water Realm at thirteen." She tilted her head with that inquisitive look in her eyes I was starting to know all too well. "Did your parents teach you? Did they have a ship?"

I turned away from her to study the door, looking for any cracks, nails, or broken hinges. "Something like that."

She paused so long I thought perhaps she'd given up, but then she asked, "Was that true, what you said the other night about your parents? And your first time?"

I looked her in the eye. "Everything I've told you is true. I may keep secrets, but I've never lied."

"I'm sorry you had to go through all that." She looked at me with the pity I'd been trying to avoid. That was why I didn't tell people this stuff. I didn't need anyone's pity, and certainly not hers.

I lifted one shoulder casually. "It was a long time ago."

"Can I ask what happened to your family?"

My lips pressed into a tight line briefly. "They were killed by the Crimson Dragon, like yours were."

Her face paled. "Why didn't you tell me?"

I looked away with a scowl. "Because I didn't want you to think this makes us connected in some way. Sark is the Black Dragon's enforcer. He's killed a lot of families. It doesn't mean anything."

"But we *are* connected, and now I understand you a

little more. Or better than I did, anyway." She rose to her feet and moved toward me with sympathy on her face. "The Dragons both took away our families. Did they think your parents were part of the Resistance too?"

"They *were* in the Resistance," I snapped. "They got themselves killed, along with everyone they cared about, all for their stupid cause."

"How is that stupid? They died for their ideals. We're fighting for the same thing now—to stop the Dragons."

I crossed my arms. "Trust me, that's not my idea. If it were up to me, we'd find a nice island to hide out on until this all blew over."

She stared at me with fire in her eyes. "You think we should run away?"

"If it saves our lives, then yes. If my family was smart, they would never have gotten involved with the Resistance —and they'd still be alive today."

She gestured wildly. "And what about all the people who will suffer if we don't stop the Dragons?"

"How is the suffering of the entire world our problem?"

"Because the Gods chose us!"

"And like I said, the Water God chose wrong."

With those words I would normally have stormed off, but all I could do was walk to the other side of our cell and face away from her. Gods, what was I even doing? And why had I come back to Kira? I had no desire to stop the Dragons or represent a God. I didn't want to be involved in this impossible fight. We were only going to get ourselves killed —including Kira.

Her small hand rested on my back and I stiffened up. "I don't think he did," she said.

I spun to face her. "You're wrong. I'm no hero. I don't care about saving the world. I don't even know why I'm still here."

Her fingers brushed against my jaw as she looked up at me in a way that made my chest clench. "I know why. Deep down you have a good heart, even if you won't admit it."

I took her beautiful face in my hands. "I've been many things in this life. A thief. A whore. A killer. But I have never once been a good man."

"It's not too late to start."

My thumb ran across her lower lip and I was seconds away from kissing her hard and showing her that I wasn't good at all, when the door opened. Kira and I jumped back as Slade was thrown into the prison with us. The door was locked again before I could even summon a shard of ice. Dammit, there went my plan of escape. If I hadn't been distracted by Kira, I'd have been ready.

"Slade!" Kira threw her arms around him. I tried to ignore that touch of jealousy twisting in my gut, along with the realization that I would have kissed her if he hadn't interrupted us.

I turned away and crossed my arms. It was better that we'd been interrupted anyway. Everyone I'd ever loved was dead, and I refused to love Kira and have her meet the same fate. But for some reason I wasn't able to walk away from her either. Gods knew I'd tried, yet here I was. Drawn by this invisible string to her side, no matter how much I wanted to fight it or escape it.

And in the end, it would probably get us both killed.

12

KIRA

I pulled back from my tight hug to examine Slade for any injuries. "Are you all right?"

He nodded as he leaned against me, his hands still bound behind his back. "They asked me some questions and roughed me up a bit, but nothing I couldn't handle. The biggest problem was that they think we kidnapped Auric."

"Of course they did," Reven muttered, as he bent down to cut the bindings on Slade's wrist.

I gestured for Slade to get on the cot and then pulled up his shirt, revealing his hard muscles and smooth dark skin. As I pressed a hand to his ribs, he inhaled sharply. He'd definitely taken a beating and would likely be black and blue soon, not to mention whatever was going on inside of him. A broken rib maybe. I closed my eyes and willed his body to heal, causing his cool skin to warm under my touch.

"What did they ask you?" Reven asked him.

Slade's eyes were closed and when he spoke it sounded pained. "They wanted to know what we were doing with Auric, how we had captured him, and why we had returned. I didn't tell them anything. I wasn't sure they'd even believe me if I did."

"Probably not," I said.

After I finished healing Slade, the door was thrown open and Jasin was pushed into the room by a guard. He stumbled forward and hit the ground on his knees, with a trail of blood trailing from his lip and his left eye puffy and swollen. Gods, what had they done to him? And why was he so much worse than Slade? Had he given them a hard time?

I rushed to Jasin's side and took his face in my hands, eager to heal him, but a gloved hand gripped my arm. I looked up at the plumed helmet of the Captain.

"Come with us," he said to me.

Two other guards stood behind him, pointing their swords at my chest. At the sight, Reven let out a low growl and summoned small blades of ice in his hands. Slade pushed himself to his feet and clenched his fists, while Jasin threw himself in front of me and growled, "Don't touch her."

A fight seemed inevitable even if I went willingly, and maybe fighting was the only way we would be able to escape and find Auric. I wished we could do it without shedding blood or revealing the secret of our magic, although I was less concerned about shedding blood after I'd seen what the guards had done to my men.

"Stop!" Auric yelled. My breath caught and relief rushed through me at the sight of him pushing through the wall of guards. As they parted, he stood tall before me, looking every inch the regal prince even in his common traveling clothes. "Let her go."

The Captain released me. "Yes, your highness."

Auric gestured at my other mates. "Release these people at once. As I told you earlier, there was no kidnapping. I left the Air Realm willingly, and these are my hired guards."

The Captain hesitated, but then nodded and stepped back so we could leave the prison cell. All of the guards sheathed their weapons, while Slade helped Jasin stand. Reven glared at the Captain as he sauntered by, making his way to my side.

We were given back our things, including all our weapons, and then escorted out of the prison into the bright afternoon sunlight. Another group of guards awaited us there, along with a gilded carriage emblazoned with the royal crest.

And just like that, we were released.

I wrapped my arms around Auric and gave him a quick kiss. "I knew you would get us out of there."

He kissed me back, but then grimaced. "Yes, I did. Unfortunately everyone knows I'm here now. Including my entire family."

"Can we get some horses and leave the city tonight?" Slade asked.

"No, I've been ordered to return to the palace, and the Royal Guard will make sure I comply." Auric glanced back at the prison, where the Captain and the other guards were watching us intently. "We have to meet with my parents before we can head for the Air Temple."

A servant opened the carriage for us, which was quite different from the one we'd traveled in earlier with no windows. This one had lush purple interior trimmed with yellow accents, all made of the finest velvet and trimmed with real gold. I sank into the cushion with Jasin and Reven at my side, with Auric and Slade across from us. Everyone except Auric was disgusting and bloody after being in the prison, not to mention hungry and tired from our ordeal.

Auric leaned back into the seat, his finely sculpted, perfectly clean face the only one who looked like it belonged here. "I'm sorry for all of that. Did they hurt you?"

"Nothing a little of Kira's touch won't fix," Jasin said, though he shifted uncomfortably in his seat. I took his hand to heal him and give him strength while the carriage began to roll forward.

"That should never have happened," Auric said. "Again, I'm sorry. Please let me know if there is anything I can do to help."

Slade grunted. "We'll be fine."

Auric sighed, leaning his head back. "Gods, this is a disaster. How am I going to explain this to my parents? I can't exactly tell them the truth, but I don't want to lie to them either."

"Keep it vague," Reven said.

"I shall. I told the guards you were mercenaries I'd hired to protect me during my travels. We'll stick to that for now, I suppose. But my family is going to have a lot of questions for me."

"Who else will we meet at the palace?" I asked. Although this wasn't how we'd hoped to spend our time in Stormhaven, I couldn't help but be curious about Auric's family and his home. I only hoped it went better for us than our meeting with Jasin's parents did.

"My mother and father. My siblings, if any of them are staying at the castle, though my oldest brother Niyal is probably at the palace in Mistvale and my sister Fema is likely on her estate with her husbands. My other brother Garet should be there though." He hesitated and opened his mouth like he wanted to say more, but then thought better of it.

While Jasin and Slade dosed off, the rest of us stared through the windows at the city as we moved through it. Everywhere I looked people were walking by in brightly colored clothing that flowed loosely and revealed plenty of skin. They stopped at little shops and adorable cafes, while above us the tall spires reached high into the sky.

The carriage climbed a hill as we approached the palace, which shined under the sun like a beacon. Auric's body was tense as we passed through a huge gate before traveling along a stone path lined with perfectly trimmed trees with tiny yellow and white flowers. I pressed my face close to the tiny window to see everything I could, filled with awe at the sight of the majestic white castle in front of us.

The carriage came to a halt in a courtyard in front of the palace. Auric stepped out first and glanced around with a tense expression, then turned to offer me a hand to help me out.

I stepped out of the carriage and gaped at the beautiful palace and all the guards and servants waiting for us, wishing that my hair was brushed, or that I wasn't covered in dirt and blood, or that I wore finer clothes. I'd never had anything very nice to begin with and I'd left most of my clothes with our horses at the Fire Temple. I supposed my dirty hunting leathers fit Auric's story that we were mercenaries, but I couldn't help but feel like an imposter standing there among such finery.

As the other men stepped out of the carriage, a beautiful woman with long black hair and smooth golden skin rode up on a glorious white horse. "Auric! You've returned!"

She dropped off her horse and smoothed her peach silk riding habit, then throw her arms around Auric. She pressed a kiss to his cheek, which gave me an uncomfortable feeling in my stomach that I tried to ignore. She could be related to Auric, perhaps a cousin or other relative, but there was something about the way she touched him that seemed familiar in a different way.

Auric has never been with a woman, I reminded myself. Though he'd certainly kissed at least one before me.

"Brin, what are you doing here at the palace?" Auric asked, sounding alarmed.

"I've been staying here for the last month, ever since you vanished. I'm so relieved you're all right." She brushed a piece of dirt off Auric's chest in a way that made me squirm.

"I was so worried when you ran off like that without a word. Made me think you might want out of our arrangement."

"Yes, about that..." He glanced over at me and cleared his throat. Brin turned toward us like she hadn't even noticed us before. Her gaze swept over us with confusion on her lovely features.

"Auric, who is this?" I asked through gritted teeth.

"This is Lady Brin of House Pashona." His face turned grim. "My betrothed."

At first I thought I must have heard Auric wrong. He couldn't be engaged to another woman...could he? But then I saw the way Brin smiled as she took Auric's arm, like they had known each other for years, and my doubts vanished. It was true. They were betrothed.

I wanted to turn and run away, to escape the heartache crushing my chest and making it hard to breathe, but there was nowhere to go. Guards surrounded us, the carriage had already rolled away, and there was no place to hide out here in the sunny courtyard. My next instinct was to yell at Auric and demand answers, but that would probably get me arrested again. All I could do was stare at this perfect, regal couple in front of me while my anguish and jealousy burned so hot I was surprised the ground didn't catch fire beneath me.

"How could you keep this from me?" I asked, my voice shaking with each word.

Auric stepped toward me, breaking free of Brin's grasp. "Kira, I can explain everything."

I shook my head and turned away, swallowing hard. Slade crossed his arms and gave Auric a stony look, while Reven leaned against a pillar and watched the scene unfold with a bored expression. Jasin rested his hand on my lower back and glared at Auric. "Is that the best you can say?"

Brin eyed us all with interest, then clasped her hands together. "I can see there's a story here, and I'm guessing it's one you don't want the entire palace staff to know about." She gave me a warm smile, then swept her gaze across my mates. "Why don't you all join me in my suite, where we can talk about this in private?"

All I wanted was to return to the boat and get away from this situation, but there was no escaping this. Auric was my future mate, and no matter how upset I was with him, I had to hear him out at least.

"All right," I said reluctantly. "Let's talk."

Brin led us inside the palace into a huge entry that was all velvet and silk, purple and gold, elegant and opulent. The front room alone practically dripped with wealth and sophistication, and I immediately felt even more out of place. Especially beside Brin, who wore clothing suitable for a princess and clearly knew the palace as if it were her own home.

How could Auric have kept something this big from me? He'd already done something like this once when he'd hid that he was a prince from me, but I'd forgiven him for that and even understood why he did it. Now I wondered how I could ever trust him again. He should have at least mentioned his betrothal to me at some point. Did he love this other woman? Was that why he'd kept it a secret?

Brin led us up a glorious white spiral staircase with a gilded handrail, then down a hallway with a soft carpeted floor that felt like I was walking on clouds. She spoke to a servant briefly to order up some tea, then swept us into a room done in pale yellow and soft pink.

Once we were all inside, Brin gestured for each of us to sit on the plush chairs and loveseats. I hesitated, worried I would dirty the elegant fabric with my clothes that had touched a prison floor not long ago, until she patted the cushion. I reluctantly sat across from her and opened my mouth to speak, but then a servant wheeled a cart into the room and we were forced to sit in awkward, tense silence while she poured us all a cup of tea. It seemed to take forever, yet at the same time I was afraid of what would happen once she finished and the truth came out.

As soon as we were alone again, Brin took a sip of tea and smiled at us. "Now we can talk."

Auric glanced between us with solemn eyes. "Kira, Brin, I owe you both apologies and explanations."

"And us," Jasin added, before he grabbed one of the small pastries off the tray and shoved it in his mouth.

"Yes, we're supposed to be a team," Slade said.

"Is it true?" I asked Auric, still hoping this was all a misunderstanding. "Is she your betrothed?"

"Yes, but it isn't what you think," Auric said quickly. "Our parents arranged our marriage when we were children, but we're not in love."

Brin laughed. "Gods, no. Auric is like a brother to me." She leaned close, like she was telling me a secret. "Besides, I prefer women."

Auric nodded. "Brin is my closest friend, and we agreed to marry since it seemed the best option to appease our parents. They expect us to marry within the noble families, and Brin is the only noble I can tolerate."

Brin playfully touched Auric's arm. "Aw, that's so sweet. You're the only man I could even imagine spending my entire life with." She turned her dazzling smile on me next. "Auric and I never planned to be exclusive with each other, and we never expected a grand romance or love of that sort. Truth be told, I only agreed to marry a man to continue the family lineage, but I fully expected to take a woman or two on the side." She glanced at my mates with amusement. "Or four."

"But why didn't you tell me?" I asked Auric.

He raked a hand through his golden hair. "I was planning to tell you, I truly was. I almost did when we were on the ship, but then we were attacked by elementals, and after that things were so chaotic... But I should have found the time. I'm truly sorry."

Brin touched my knee lightly. "If he was with you, I doubt he was thinking about me at all."

"Maybe, but it doesn't change the fact that your families

expect you to marry." I gave Auric a pointed look. "And we have...other duties."

"Is that so?" Brin asked, arching one of her perfect eyebrows at Auric. "Does this have to do with why you disappeared for a month?"

"Yes, but I can't tell you more than that," he said. "I'm sorry, Brin, but I can't marry you. My path is with Kira, as is my heart."

She let out a dramatic sigh. "It's quite all right. Mom and Dad will be furious, but I'm happy you found someone you love."

Auric took my hand in his. "Kira, I'm so sorry I never told you about Brin. There were so many other more pressing things to deal with on our journey so far, and I rarely thought about my previous life here at all. But I should have told you about this and found a better way to handle all it in advance."

"Yes, you should have." I pulled my hand away, unable to hide the bitterness in my voice, and Jasin rubbed my back in support. Auric might be sorry, but would he have ever told me about Brin if we hadn't been forced to come to the palace? Was he hiding anything else? How would I ever know?

"This is why you didn't want to return to Stormhaven," Slade said. He'd remained standing along with Reven, and they both watched Auric with stony expressions.

"One of the reasons, yes." Auric stared at his hands, his face pained. "My parents won't be pleased with me ending the engagement, but there's no other option. In fact, I should probably meet with them now and tell them the news. They've no doubt heard that I'm in the palace and will be expecting me."

"They've been looking for you all over the kingdom and have been worried sick," Brin said. "Your brother Garet has been in Thundercrest all this time looking for you. I hope you have a good explanation."

He swallowed. "Not exactly."

"Better come up with one quickly then." Brin studied the five of us and tapped her red lips. "For now, we need to get you all some new clothes. We can't have you meeting the royal family looking like you just rolled out of the sewer."

"I can get some clothes for me and the other men from my quarters," Auric said, rising to his feet.

"And I should have something that should fit Kira," Brin said.

My mates grumbled, but they followed Auric out of the suite, leaving me alone with Brin. She took my arm and led me into another room. "Come now, let's get you ready to meet with the King and Queen."

I reluctantly followed her and watched while she began going through her wardrobe. "You don't need to do this..."

"Nonsense. It's my honor to help the woman who's captured Auric's heart." She pulled out a pale green gown that was finer than anything I'd ever owned and held it up to me. "Oh yes, this will be perfect on you with your beautiful red hair."

"Brin, I—"

"I insist you take this dress as a small gift from me to

apologize for any pain I've brought you." She thrust the gown at me. "Besides, the King and Queen are waiting and you must look your best."

I hesitated, then took the luxurious silken dress from her. It was thin, like most of the clothes the people wore in the Air Realm, and would cling to my body. It was beautiful, and I couldn't exactly meet the royal family dressed as I was in my dirty, worn hunting leathers, but I was reluctant to accept it. Even when Brin beamed and began searching for shoes to go with the gown.

I didn't want anything to do with Brin. I didn't want to accept her gifts or spend a single second longer in her presence. I wanted to hate her for having a claim on Auric, but that was hard when she was being so friendly and kind. It wasn't her fault that Auric had kept their betrothal from me, and she was trying to help me.

So I swallowed my pain, clutched the dress close to my aching heart, and simply said, "Thank you."

14

AURIC

Gods, I was an idiot. I should have told Kira about Brin back when we were on the boat. Or when she'd found out I was a prince. Or from the very beginning. Now I wasn't sure I would ever be able to regain Kira's trust, even though Brin had never been anything more than a friend. We would have had a marriage of convenience and nothing more, and after meeting Kira I'd already planned on ending the betrothal as soon as I could. I only wished I'd handled the situation better. I'd thought I would have more time, and never expected Brin would be staying here at the palace. Now I realized I'd just been trying to put off the inevitable as long as possible, like a fool. And I might have lost Kira because of it.

Would she even want to bond with me once we reached the Air Temple? Or would she want someone else to be the Golden Dragon now? Somehow I would have to win her over again. And I would do it, no matter how long it took or what I had to do. But right now we had more immediate problems—like my parents.

After I'd found proper attire for myself and Kira's other mates, we met up with her at the top of the grand staircase. Kira wore a pale green silk gown that accentuated her strong, feminine body, and it was hard to tear my eyes away. She nodded at me, and the five of us descended the staircase and continued toward the back of the palace.

Although this was my home and everything about it was familiar, walking through these halls was strange now. Even my clothing felt stiff and awkward compared to the clothes I'd worn while traveling. I supposed it was because I was different—no longer a prince who spent his time in the library and avoiding balls, but a warrior who had traveled three of the Realms, could control air itself, and would soon become a Dragon...if Kira still wanted me.

A servant informed me that my parents weren't in their main receiving room, but in the private garden where my father often met with close friends and family when the weather was nice. Stepping outside and breathing in the scent of the flowers and the sea air filled me with nostalgia for when I'd played in these gardens as a child with my siblings. The palace might be known for its impossibly-tall shining spires, but the lush gardens had always been one of my favorite places as a child, including the one surrounded by a hedge where my family now waited.

As we approached, I heard raised voices and spotted someone standing with my parents through the hedge: a man with pale skin and black hair tied back in a severe pony-tail, who instantly sent terror down my spine. I'd met him officially only once, but I'd seen him in the palace a handful of other times. I'd always been afraid of him, but that was nothing compared to the panic I felt now.

At first I worried he was there for us, but then Isen, the Golden Dragon, stared down my father with a sneer on his lips. "Are you telling me no?"

My father's face was stoic. "Of course not. I'm telling you it will take time."

"Time is the only luxury we do not have right now," Isen snapped.

The King spread his hands. "We're doing the best we can."

"Somehow I doubt that. Meet these demands, or you won't like the consequences." Isen's eyes shifted to my mother almost threateningly. "And neither will your people."

His form shimmered and then grew, quickly becoming a large reptilian beast with a long tail, large wings, and sharp talons and fangs. He darted into the air with barely a flap of his wings, his golden scales flashing bright under the sun.

"What's he doing here?" Jasin asked, his voice barely above a whisper.

Kira's eyes widened. "Is he looking for us?"

"I don't think so," I said. "It seems he's visiting the King for other reasons."

"Does he visit often?" Slade asked.

"Not often, but I've seen him many times over the

years," I said. "Think of it this way. If Sark is the Black Dragon's enforcer, then Isen is her ambassador. He deals with the nobility, which mostly means keeping us in line and making sure we are loyal. Sometimes the Black Dragon decrees new laws and regulations, and he's the one who makes sure the rulers carry them out."

"You've met him before?" Kira asked.

"Yes, once. He's never very friendly." I drew in a breath and glanced back at my parents, who had sat at the table under a flowering olive tree and were speaking quietly to each other. "Are you ready to speak with my parents?"

Kira wouldn't meet my eyes. "No, but what choice do we have?"

I nodded, sharing her sentiment, and steeled myself before stepping forward into the patio where my parents were sitting. Both of them had the lush golden hair so prized in the Air Realm, and I'd gotten my gray eyes from my mother and my height from my father. At the sight of me, both of them jumped to their feet.

"Auric!" my mother cried out. She crossed the distance between us and threw her arms around me. "Where have you been all this time?"

"Son," my father said, resting a heavy hand on my shoulder. His disapproving eyes seemed to pierce right to my soul, seeing all my secrets, judging my actions, and finding me wanting. It was like being a kid all over again and realizing I was in deep trouble. "We're so glad you've returned. But we have a lot of questions."

"I'm sure you do," I said. "I've been traveling across the Realms, but I'm back now, at least for a short while."

"I'm so relieved you're safe, but who are these people with you?" the Queen asked, looking past me.

"These are my...friends and traveling companions. May I introduce Kira, Reven, Jasin, and Slade. And these are my parents, King Terel and Queen Hala."

Kira dropped to a curtsy, while the men beside her bowed. "Your majesties."

My parents looked suitably confused at being introduced to commoners, but managed to nod at them in return, though my father couldn't hide the pinch of his forehead. "I think it's time you told us where you've been all this time," he said.

Under his stony eyes I found I couldn't lie, and I couldn't come up with a good excuse. "I'm sorry, but I can't tell you."

"What do you mean, can't?" the King said.

My mother's eyes widened. "Were you captured? Held against your will? Truly, you can tell us anything. We'll love you no matter what."

"No, I left the Air Realm of my own free will." Gods, this was harder than I'd expected. I wracked my brain for a way to explain without telling them the whole truth. "I needed to get away from the palace and find my place in the world.

"But why didn't you tell us?" the Queen asked. "We were so worried."

"Because you would have tried to stop me, or would

have sent guards with me. This was something I needed to do alone, but I'm sorry I made you worry. As you can see, I'm perfectly fine."

My father's frown deepened. "Does this have anything to do with your engagement to Brin?"

I cleared my throat. "Yes, in a way. I'm sorry, but I can't marry Brin anymore."

"Why ever not?" my mother asked.

I took Kira's hand in mine. "Because I've given my heart to another, and my future is with her."

Now I'd truly shocked them. For a moment they were both speechless, and then my mother pressed a hand to her chest and asked the others, "Would you mind giving us a moment to speak to our son alone?"

"Yes, of course," Kira said, as she met my eyes with a frown. I doubted she wanted to be here anyway after everything that had happened in the last few hours. I couldn't count on the other men to back me up either. I had to face my parents alone.

A servant whisked Kira and her other mates away, and as soon as they were gone my mother asked, "You wish to marry that...commoner?"

I bowed my head. "I do."

"No," my father said. "I forbid it."

My heart sank, but my resolve strengthened. "I'm sorry, but I'm going to be with Kira whether you like it or not."

He shook his head. "Son, you barely know this woman. Where is she even from? And who were those other three men?"

"It's complicated—"

"How do you know she doesn't only want you because you're a prince?" the Queen asked.

I raked a hand through my hair, frustrated with this questioning. Couldn't they trust that I wouldn't be with someone like that? "She didn't know I was a prince at first. She doesn't care about my money or status at all."

"I find that hard to believe," the King said. He sat in one of the patio chairs and gestured for me to do the same. "Tell us everything about her, along with a detailed account of your travels over the last few weeks."

I sank into the chair with a sigh. I could already tell was going to be a long night.

Wﻬ hile Auric spoke in private with his parents, we
were taken to another small sitting room where
supper was brought to us. I tried not to devour all of it
within seconds, and I noticed my mates were eating just as
quickly. None of us had eaten since we'd been on the boat in
the morning, and for days we'd been living off of old bread
and fish, plus whatever else Calla and her mates had left for
us on the boat. It was a nice change to have someone else
cook for us, and the food was exquisite—chicken roasted in a
crisp lemon sauce with peppers and onions in oil and garlic,
plus fresh bread, soft cheese, and olives. It was said the
cuisine in the Air Realm was the best in the world, and
tonight I thought that might be true.

The men kept stealing glances at me as we ate and asked
numerous times if I was okay, but all I could do was nod. I
simply couldn't find the energy to speak about what had

happened in the last few hours with Auric. I needed some time alone to go over my thoughts and emotions before making a decision about what we would do next.

After we finished eating I was shown to my room, and I was so physically and emotionally exhausted I wanted nothing more than to collapse onto the bed and pass out. But when I stepped inside, the room was so beautiful it made me hesitate to touch anything. The room was done in sky blue and soft cream, making me feel like I was outside under an endless sky. In the center stood a huge four-poster bed, much larger and fancier than anything I'd slept in before, with more pillows than I'd seen in my life. Truly, how could anyone need that many pillows? I could construct an entire new bed out of them.

Large windows on either side of the bed looked out at the ocean from behind some soft curtains, and there was also a small sitting area, dresser, and wardrobe. All of it was so beautiful and luxurious that it only served as a reminder that I didn't belong here...or with Auric. Meeting his parents and Brin had made that clear. I'd immediately seen the disdain in his parents' eyes when Auric announced he wanted to be with me, and after meeting Brin, I understood why—she was what they wanted for their son, and I had to admit it made more sense for them to be together.

How could I have thought his being a prince didn't matter? We'd lived completely different lives. He'd grown up in a castle with servants waiting on him hand and foot. I'd been on the run for years, taking whatever jobs I could to earn money. Auric should be with someone who understood this life, not me.

Besides, I was still mad at him. I wasn't sure I would ever be able to trust him again after he'd kept so many things from me. Maybe it would be best for all of us if we parted ways now and he went back to his old life. But then who would be my Golden Dragon?

The Golden Dragon... I'd seen the current one tonight for the first time and he'd instantly set me on edge. He'd been right there—if he had turned around, would he have realized who we were? And what did he want from Auric's parents?

As my thoughts churned, I allowed myself to sink onto the edge of the bed and drop my head in my hands. We'd come so close to ruin today in so many ways, it was no wonder I was exhausted. Maybe I'd be able to sort through all my tangled thoughts after I'd had a bit of sleep.

Someone knocked on my door. I slowly moved to open it and was surprised to find Slade standing on the other side. "My room is right next to yours in case you need anything," he said. "Are you all right?"

"Not really. I'm tired, overwhelmed, upset..." I shrugged helplessly. "But I'll be fine in the morning."

He rested his hands on my upper arms. "You don't have to be strong all the time, Kira. It's okay to cry or yell or break down. That's why you have us. We're here for you to lean on."

Tears filled my eyes at his words, which touched me deep to my core. "Thank you. For so many years I relied on no one but myself. I'm not used to having other people I can turn to for help or support. Except Tash, I suppose."

His thumbs slowly rubbed my arms. "You miss her?"

"Very much. I wish she were here. I'd love to have another girl to talk to about all this."

"Brin seemed nice enough."

My nose scrunched up. "Yes, but that only makes it harder. It would be so much easier if I could hate her. Besides, she's the one I want to talk about!"

He let out a low chuckle. "Maybe you can send a letter to Tash to let her know you're safe. It might make you feel better."

A smile touched my lips for the first time in hours. "That's a great idea. I'll write it in the morning and tell Auric to make sure it gets delivered to her. He owes me that, at least."

He nodded. "I know we're your mates and that makes things complicated. But don't forget, we're your friends too."

"And I'm lucky to have you." I sighed and leaned against the doorway. "Well, some of you. I'm not feeling very lucky to have Auric right now."

Slade ran a hand over his dark beard as he chose his next words. "Auric made a mistake, it's true. But we're all doing the best we can with this situation we've been put in. We each have pasts we'd like to forget, or things we're trying to run from. At least he is facing it now."

"That doesn't excuse him keeping this from me."

"No, it doesn't." His large, dark hand cupped my cheek

and I thought he might kiss me for the first time, but then he turned away. "Get some rest, Kira."

I stared after Slade as he slipped into his room, then closed my own door. Would he ever see me as more than a friend? I was grateful for his friendship, I truly was, but I wanted more too. Someday. I wouldn't rush him, even if I couldn't stop thinking about how much I wanted him to kiss me. Did he feel that invisible tug between us too, trying to bring our bodies together? Or was I the only one?

16

KIRA

In the morning I found myself restless and unsure of what to do or where to go in the palace. What was my role here? And how long would we stay before continuing on to the Air Temple? While it was nice to have some time to rest and recover from our travels, every second we delayed increased the likelihood of the Dragons uncovering who we were or reaching the temple before us.

Jasin suggested we take this time to train, and while the idea of using fire would have previously terrified me, today I really needed to burn some of my anxious energy off.

The palace was nestled on a tall hill overlooking the city on one side and the ocean on the other, and Jasin and I trekked out to the end of the bluff overlooking the water, where the blue sky seemed endless. The bright sun warmed us as we stared down the edge of the steep, rocky cliff that disappeared into the ocean below us.

"This will do," Jasin said, glancing around at the sparse trees and rocks.

I inched away from the drop. "Isn't it a bit close to the edge?"

Jasin shrugged. "If you fall, I'll catch you. Don't forget I can turn into a dragon now."

"Sorry, but I'm not that confident in your flying skills yet."

"All right, we can move back a bit. I suppose it would be hard to explain why an unknown Dragon was flying near the palace." He moved to a safer location and spread his arms. "Let's see what you can do."

I summoned a small ball of fire and threw it at Jasin, who swept it away with an easy gesture. "How is that?"

"Not bad at all. You're a natural. Which is surprising since you were scared of fire only days ago."

"I leaned by watching you, I suppose." Truth be told, I was still scared of fire and what it could do, but I had to get over it. And I could only do that with practice and training.

"Then you know that fire is the hardest element to keep control of. Summoning it is easy. But making it do what you want...that's the real challenge. I'm still learning that part myself." He pointed at a nearby shrubby bush and it instantly caught fire, but the blaze didn't spread to anything else. Jasin's face pinched as he concentrated, and I could tell it took a lot of effort to keep it contained. Then the fire vanished in a blast of smoke. "For now, let's just have you concentrate on throwing the fire and making sure it goes where you want it to go."

Jasin hurled a ball of fire at a nearby boulder, where it flashed and then disappeared with nothing to keep it burning. I nodded and summoned my own flames, then tossed them at the stone. As I did, the events of yesterday came back to me, including everything I'd been trying very hard not to think about, like Auric and how he'd kept the truth about Brin from me. I still cared for him, but how was I supposed to trust him now? Or bond with him in only a few days?

I tossed a huge ball of fire, enjoying the sizzle and the flash of heat. "This is exactly what I needed."

"Of course it is. Fire is all about passion. Anger, desire, excitement... When you channel these emotions, you'll find it easier to conjure fire." He tilted his head. "I get the sense you're definitely feeling some passion today."

I wiped the sweat off my forehead. "Anger, mostly. I trusted Auric and he kept a huge secret from me for the second time. How am I supposed to just accept that and move on now?"

"That's understandable. But we're all keeping things from each other. I didn't tell you about my brother's death, or that my parents were staunch supporters of the Dragons, Sark in particular. In fact, I purposefully kept that to myself because I couldn't stand to talk about it and I worried what you would think. Maybe Auric felt the same way about his engagement?"

I stared at Jasin. "Are you defending him?"

He held up his hands. "No, definitely not."

"Good, because his secret is different. I can't be with a man who is engaged to another."

Jasin shrugged. "It sounds like their betrothal was more for show or convenience than love, and he told his parents he wanted to be with you instead."

I summoned another ball of flame and rolled it around in my palms. "Maybe so, but it was still there all this time. I wish he would have told me from the beginning."

"For what it's worth, I think Auric loves you and you alone. You have every right to be mad at him, but I don't think Brin is a threat. Their engagement will end, and soon we'll be on our way to the Air Temple."

I glanced away, annoyed at how reasonable Jasin was being. Wasn't he normally the hotheaded one of the group? And why was he defending Auric when only days ago they'd hated each other? I knew I would have to forgive Auric and move past this somehow, but at the moment all I wanted was to let out my anger and smash things—or burn them.

I launched my next fireball, but it was bigger than I expected and went wide, hitting a large bush, which instantly went up in flames. The fire quickly leaped to a tree beside it and spread faster than I could have imagined, sending cold panic down my spine. Flashbacks of the fire that had taken my parents' lives flickered in my head as my heart pounded and my breathing grew ragged. I couldn't think, couldn't move, couldn't stop it.

"Get back!" Jasin stepped forward and gestured at the fire. His face was tight with concentration as he soothed the flames and contained them, then slowly made them smaller and smaller.

After a few minutes there was nothing but ash and smoke where the tree had been. I'd completely destroyed it, and I'd lost all control of the fire. I sank to the grass and stared at the charred ground, feeling empty and hollow. What if I'd lost control during battle? Or in a crowded area with people and houses? I could have killed someone. I could have destroyed innocent lives. How could I use fire when it had so much potential for destruction and pain?

Jasin sat beside me on the grass and began slowly rubbing my back. "It's over. You're fine."

"It's not fine. I lost control." I covered my face with my hands, which were still trembling.

"I did too, at first. Remember when Reven had to put out all my fires?" He pulled me close. "You just need more practice, that's all."

I nodded and buried my face against his shoulder, but if I was honest, I didn't want to practice my magic ever again. I didn't want that kind of power or responsibility. Even now, I couldn't help but think this was all a mistake and someone else should be the Black Dragon. How was I supposed to master all four elements when I couldn't even handle one?

17

REVEN

I n the morning I slipped out of the palace, unnoticed by any guards or servants, and headed back into the city. Stormhaven was already waking up even as dawn crested over the ocean waves to the east, a sight that always seemed wrong to me. The sun should be setting *into* the water, as it did in the Water Realm, not rising from it.

I moved through the brightening streets with my hood up, a shadow among the bustling crowds headed for the markets and shops. As the day heated up, I made my way to the docks, where the air smelled of salt and fish, while sailors hauled crates onto the ships. Our boat waited at the northern end, and though Auric had said he'd sorted everything out with the guard, I wanted to confirm it with my own eyes to make sure we had a quick exit strategy, especially since we didn't have our horses with us. All good assassins had at least three exits planned out in case something went wrong...and something always went wrong.

A royal guard was perched in front of our boat, but I had no interest in giving her an explanation to as to why I was there. When no one was looking, I dropped off the dock and slipped into the water, feeling the instant relief as the chill surrounded me. As the Azure Dragon's ascendant I could breathe underwater, and I easily swam over to the other side of the boat. I climbed up the outside of it while using my magic to remove the water from my clothes and send it back into the ocean. By the time I vaulted up onto the wooden deck I was completely dry and the royal guard didn't have a clue I was there.

From up here, everything seemed to be in order. I dropped down into the hatch leading below deck, and found evidence that the guards had tossed the place, probably looking for something incriminating so they could pin Auric's supposed kidnapping on us, or perhaps find an explanation as to where he'd been all this time. Our things had been taken during the search and had been delivered last night to us in the palace, but I checked a few nooks and crannies to make sure nothing had been left behind, then removed the spare knife I'd hidden under one of the wooden planks. Finally, I rearranged the hammock and cleaned up some of the other mess, before climbing back up.

As I walked off the ship, I gave the confused guard a nod. She called out some questions, but didn't follow me more than a few feet. Probably on orders to stay with the ship at all times. I turned a corner and left her behind.

It had been a year since I'd been in Stormhaven, but it hadn't changed much. People wore colorful, loose clothing, and the bustling crowd was ripe for pickpocketing. Cafes and little shops sold everything from clothes to art to pastries. For a split second I considered buying something for Kira to cheer her up after what Auric had done, but then dismissed the idea entirely. I wasn't trying to woo her. We weren't a couple. If I was smart, I'd just keep walking and never return to the castle at all.

Maybe that was why I ended up in a seedy neighborhood where the crowd didn't dare wander. A dark, unmarked building was tucked at the end of an alley, and I slipped inside. The tavern was otherwise empty this early in the day, and the bartender gave me a nod as I sat at the end of the bar. She had short, white hair and a tattoo of a dagger on her wrinkled neck, and though she didn't look like much of a threat, I knew better.

Zara poured me some ale. "Surprised to see you, Reven. Last I heard you weren't taking on any jobs at the moment."

I pushed my hood back. "I took some time off."

She nodded. "Always a good idea now and then. Don't want to get burned out. This is a tough profession."

My eyes narrowed. Me, burn out? Was that was others in the Guild thought? I took a long sip of the cold ale and then said, "I'm here now."

"That so?" She wiped down the counter as she eyed me with scrutiny. "As it turns out, a job came in last night that requires a special touch."

"My specialty."

"This one is high profile, with the biggest reward I've seen in all my days. Won't be easy though. Might be too much for even you."

"I doubt that." I gestured for her to get on with it. "What's the job?"

She leaned over the counter and dropped her voice. "The target is the King."

"The King," I said, my voice flat. "Why would someone want him dead?"

"I don't know. The order came from above." Her eyes flicked to the ceiling. "Way above."

"A Dragon?"

"I can't say any more." She refilled my drink and sighed. "The King is well loved here in Stormhaven and his reign has been a good one. It's a damn shame. But we can't exactly say no to the Dragons."

I tightened my grip on the glass. "No, we can't."

"Are you interested?" Zara asked. "Or should I find someone else?"

I chugged my ale as I considered, realizing this moment would define my path for the rest of my life. Zara was giving me the chance to return to my old life and prove to the Guild I was still the best. It would require killing Auric's father and serving the Dragons, but wasn't that who I was—an assassin for hire? I'd already walked away from Kira once. I could do it again, and this time it would be permanent. Or I could walk away from my past and accept my fate with Kira as the next Azure Dragon.

I set down my ale and met Zara's eyes. "I'll take the job."

18

KIRA

After my training with Jasin I returned to my room to take my midday meal alone with my thoughts. As I picked at the cod cooked with tomatoes and onions, I composed a letter to Tash telling her everything we had experienced so far, while trying to keep my wording vague enough that no one would know what our plans were if the letter got into the wrong hands.

The letter ended up being two pages front and back because once I started talking to Tash in my head I couldn't stop. I told her about Jasin's family and about Auric's fiancé. I told her about how Slade was distant and Reven had left for a short time. I told her about the weight of the responsibility that had been pressed upon me and my fears I would never become the leader I was supposed to be. And even though Tash wouldn't read my letter for some time, a great weight was lifted off me simply by writing it.

A knock sounded on my door and I called out for them to enter. As I folded up the letter and put it in an envelope, Auric stepped inside. My stomach twisted at the sight of him lingering in the doorway as if he wasn't sure he was truly welcome. He'd returned to his fine nobleman's clothing, his face had been shaved, and his golden hair had been cut short again. He looked every inch the handsome prince that he was, even though I'd liked his rougher traveling look too. I suspected the true Auric was somewhere between the two extremes.

"Can we talk, Kira?" he asked.

"Yes, I'm just finishing up a letter to my friend Tash back in Stoneham. Would it be possible to have it delivered to her?"

"Of course." He held out his palm and I set the letter in it. "I'll send a messenger right away."

"Thank you." I couldn't help but notice how stiff we were around each other and didn't like this new tension between us, even though I was still upset with him. "What did you want to talk about?"

His storm gray eyes stared into mine. "My engagement with Brin is over. We met with her parents this morning to make it official."

I let out a long breath. "That's a relief."

"Yes. Everyone is quite upset with me, but I've never been a very dutiful son or prince, so it's to be expected I guess. And soon we'll be gone anyway."

"When can we leave for the Air Temple?"

"Soon, but I need another day or two to appease my

parents. My mother insists on throwing us a ball before we go."

My eyebrows darted up and anxiety fluttered in my stomach. "A ball?"

"Yes, to celebrate my safe return, however short it may be, but you don't need to worry. It will be drinking, dancing, and lots of food, and then we can leave for the Air Temple the next day." He cleared his throat. "That is, if you still want me to go to the Air Temple with you."

"I do," I said without hesitation. Though I was upset with Auric, he was still the one I wanted as my mate. The second he'd walked into my room I'd known that for sure.

"Thank the Gods." A smile lit up his face and he offered me his hand. "There's somewhere I'd like to show you. Will you come with me?"

I took his hand and he led me out of my room, down the great staircase, and along a hallway, where we reached two double doors. As he threw one open, I gasped. Inside was the giant library I'd glimpsed in my dreams when I'd first seen Auric. Every wall was covered in shelves that were packed tight with books of all shapes and colors. I'd never seen so many books before in my life, as they were rare treasures in most of the places I'd lived before.

One wall held gigantic windows that looked out at the ocean in the distance, and Auric led me to a small sitting area in front of them.

"This room is gorgeous," I said, as I sat on one of the plush couches.

Auric sat beside me on the same couch, our knees

touching as he turned toward me. "It's my favorite place in the palace, and where I usually spend most of my days."

"I know. This is where I saw you in my dreams, though I only caught a few glimpses." I gazed in awe at all the tall shelves. "I'm glad I got to see it in person."

"Me too. I was nervous about coming to the palace, but I'm actually happy you met my family and saw my home, even if the circumstances could have been better. That's my fault, I know."

"I'm pleased I got to meet them too, although I doubt they will ever like me or accept me. And I'm still upset with you."

"I know, and I'm sorry. I should have told you long ago so that you knew what awaited us when we arrived in Stormhaven, and so you knew that the betrothal was not important to me." He took my hands in his and gazed into my eyes. "You're the one I love, Kira. From the moment we met I knew there would never be anyone else. I only hope you can forgive me for my mistakes. I never meant to lie to you or hurt you."

My heart thumped faster in my chest at his words. "I know you didn't, but it will still take some time for me to trust you again."

"I can live with that, as long as you still want me to be your Golden Dragon?"

"I do, although I can't help but question why you want the role. We come from such different lives. I'd managed to forget that while we were traveling, but being at the palace and meeting your family and Brin only showed me that maybe we don't belong together."

His brow furrowed. "Kira, you know I don't care about any of that."

I remembered the way the King and Queen had looked at me when Auric had said he wanted to be with me instead of Brin, and a hard pit formed in my stomach. "I'm a commoner. I've been poor and on the run most of my life. You're a *prince*. Your family will never accept me."

He squeezed my hands. "You may have started life as a commoner, but you're going to be the Black Dragon. Someday you'll be more powerful than any King or Queen."

I yanked my hands away, my stomach twisting. "Is that why you want to be the Golden Dragon? For the power?"

"No, not at all." He raked a hand through his shining blond hair. "Gods, I'm really messing up this apology. I want to be the Golden Dragon because I love you and can't imagine not being by your side. But also because I've seen what the Dragons have done to the world, especially these past few weeks we've been traveling. I've watched my parents try to subtly resist them for years, but they're unable to do much to defy the Dragons. For years I was the odd prince who had no real importance or role in the kingdom, and for the first time ever I have a purpose. With you, I can do my part to make the world better. That's what I want."

"But you could stay here as a prince, living a safe, calm life as a scholar and a husband to your friend. If you go with us, you'll be in danger every day."

He touched my cheek lightly. "I would rather be in

danger and be by your side, trying to make the world better, than stay here in safety. All I want is to be your Golden Dragon, if you'll still have me."

I couldn't help but lean into his touch. "You're still one of my mates, Auric. And though I forgive you, I need some time before I trust you again."

"I understand, and I swear I'm not hiding anything else. This is it." He spread his arms wide. "And for what it's worth, I think you'll like Brin too, if you give her a chance."

"Maybe. If I can get over the urge to stake my claim on you every time she's around."

"Well, I won't argue if you want to do that." He leaned close, his eyes turning stormy. "In fact, maybe you should do that now, in case she's watching."

The hint of a smile touched my lips, and I couldn't deny the desire that flickered inside me when he was this close. "You're impossible."

"Jasin might be rubbing off on me."

"He told me to forgive you earlier, when we were training."

"Did he? Maybe I'm rubbing off on *him*." Auric brushed his thumb along my lips, his eyes searching mine. I parted my lips for him, taking his thumb into my mouth, and sucked gently. He let out a groan and then cupped my face in his hands and pressed his mouth to mine. I kissed him back roughly, our tongues dancing together, my hands sliding around his neck to pull him closer. I poured all my anger, doubts, and fears into this kiss, and he held me tight, like he was scared to let go.

"I worried I'd never kiss you again," he said, pressing his forehead against mine.

The doors flew open, making us both jump and pull apart. Reven stormed inside, his black hooded cloak trailing behind him. "I had a feeling you'd be in here. We need to talk."

I smoothed my dress, my cheeks warm. "Is something wrong?"

"Yes. The Golden Dragon has ordered the assassination of the King and Queen."

Auric's eyes widened. "How do you know?"

"Because I just took the job." Reven held up a hand. "Don't worry, I'm not going to do it."

"Then why did you take it?" I asked.

Reven crossed his arms. "Because if I didn't, someone else would."

"But what will happen if you don't do it?"

"They'll probably send someone to kill me too. Either way, I'll never be able to find work with the Assassin's Guild again." He gave a casual shrug. "I was ready to get out of the business anyway."

"Thank you," Auric said. "I appreciate you doing this for us."

Reven's face darkened. "The Dragons destroyed my family. They murdered Kira's family too. I can't let them do this anymore. Not to you. Not to anyone."

I jumped up and threw my arms around Reven. "I knew you were one of us."

"I wouldn't go that far," Reven muttered, though he reluctantly draped his arms around me.

"We need to speak with my parents immediately," Auric said.

I nodded, but then I had an idea. It was risky, but if the current Dragons wanted Auric's parents dead, perhaps they could be allies to us. Besides, I was tired of all the secrets and lies. "I think it's time we told them the truth about why you left."

19

KIRA

We summoned Jasin and Slade, while Auric asked for a meeting with his parents. A short time later we were led to a small parlor decorated in purple and gold, with small flaky pastries and tea already waiting for us.

"This is a bad idea," Jasin muttered, as we sat down.

"My gut tells me this is the right thing to do," I said. One thing I'd learned from a life on the run was to trust my gut, even when it was full of nervous energy, like now.

"I agree with Kira," Slade said. "No more secrets."

Reven leaned against the wall instead of joining us on the sofas. "There are always more secrets."

The King stormed into the room with his tall, commanding presence, followed by his wife and Auric. King Terel swept his gaze across the room and asked, "What is this about? My son says you have something to tell me?"

Reven stepped forward and swept into a low, graceful

bow. "Your majesty, I'm a member of the Assassin's Guild. Today I met with a local contact to gather news and check in, but once there, I was offered a job: to end your life."

King Terel's eyes narrowed at Reven. "Why are you telling me this?"

"Because the one who ordered the assassination was none other than the Golden Dragon."

The King's hands clenched into fists. "That snake."

"Would Isen really do such a thing?" Queen Hala asked.

"It seems so," Reven said.

"Why would the Dragons want you dead?" Auric asked.

"Isen has been pushing me to conduct regular raids and public executions on the Resistance members, but I refuse," King Terel said. "I won't have my people living in fear all the time, or turn death into a spectacle."

"That's what they do in the Fire Realm," Jasin said.

The King nodded. "So I've heard. But here in the Air Realm we value freedom and peace."

"Do you support the Resistance?" I asked.

The King turned his intimating gaze on me. "No, but we have ordered our guards and the Onyx Army here to look the other way on their activities sometimes. Still, I can't imagine the Dragons wanting me dead over that. What will my death accomplish?"

"The Dragons probably believe your heir would be easier to manipulate," Slade said.

King Terel rubbed his chin. "If so, they're right. Niyal's wife is pregnant with their first child. He'd do anything to protect them."

"What are we going to do?" Queen Hala asked with a sigh. "We can't give in to Isen's demands."

"Once the Assassin's Guild realizes I've failed in my assignment, they'll send someone else," Reven said. "You might want to leave the city and go somewhere safer for now."

King Terel snorted. "I won't hide. This is my kingdom and my home. Let them try to take me down."

"And I'm staying with you," Queen Hala said, as she took his hand.

He looked into her eyes and his face softened. "My love, it isn't safe. You should join Niyal at the palace in Mistvale."

She shook her head. "You're the one they want dead. I'm not leaving your side. But how can we end this? We can't openly defy the Dragons."

"Not yet, but that might change soon," Auric said.

King Terel turned toward him. "How so?"

Auric drew in a breath and straightened up. "Mother, father, there is no easy way to say this, but new Dragons have been chosen by the Gods. The five of us."

"New Dragons?" King Terel asked with a frown. "Is that possible?"

"It was surprising to us too, but it's true," Auric continued. "That's why I had to leave suddenly, to find Kira, who will one day be the Black Dragon. And it's why we must leave again in a few days to head to the Air Temple so that I can become the Golden Dragon."

Queen Hala blinked at her son. "I'm sorry, I don't quite understand. How can you be a Dragon?"

"I'm not a Dragon yet," Auric explained patiently. "That's why I need to head to the Air Temple."

"But how did this happen?" she asked, sounding completely baffled.

"The Air God came to me and chose me. I don't really know why."

King Terel crossed his arms. "Son, this all sounds very far-fetched. I'm not sure what game you're playing at, but I don't think it's helping the situation."

"We need to show them," Jasin said.

"Here?" I asked. "Now?"

"When else?" He opened his hand and a bright flame flickered into life, making the royals gasp.

Slade lifted a wooden table three feet in the air, while Reven grumbled but conjured water in front of us. Finally, Auric created a strong wind that lifted all the papers off the table and made them fly around the room before landing again in a pile in front of the King, whose mouth hung open.

"I know this is hard to believe, but it's the truth," Auric said. "We're going to be the next Dragons, and Kira here is the future Black Dragon."

"This is incredible," King Terel said. "I didn't realize the Dragons could be replaced. I thought they were eternal."

"Everyone does," I said. "But we recently learned that the Dragons were only supposed to rule for a short while before being replaced, to make sure they never became too powerful. The current Dragons somehow found a way around that and have wiped out any trace of the previous Dragons' existence."

"You said the Air God came to you?" Queen Hala asked her son. "And gave you these powers?"

Auric nodded. "Yes, outside in the courtyard one morning. He chose me, though I'm still not sure why."

She rested her hand on his shoulder. "You should have told us this from the beginning instead of running off without a word. We were all so worried about you."

"The Air God instructed me not to tell anyone. Besides, would you have believed me?"

She sighed. "No. I hardly believe it now."

He patted his mother's hand. "And now you see why I had to end my engagement with Brin. My destiny is with Kira and her other mates. We need to visit each of the temples to unlock our powers, and then we'll be able to challenge the Dragons. Do we have your support?"

"I'll do whatever I can to help," King Terel said.

"But what will we do about this assassination?" the Queen asked.

"Spread word that an attack was made but the assassin was defeated," Reven said. "That will buy you some time, at least."

"You may have to pretend to go along with the Golden Dragon's demands for a while," Auric said. "Until we can be sure the family is safe."

The King nodded. "It pains me to do such a thing, but I suppose I can have my guards do a few harmless searches for Resistance members. I'm putting my foot down on public executions though."

"When do you need to leave for the Air Temple?" Queen Hala asked.

"As soon as possible," I said.

She nodded. "We'll begin preparations immediately for your departure, but you must stay for the ball. I insist."

Auric bowed his head. "We'll attend the ball, but then we're leaving the next morning."

"It's settled then," the King said, rising to his full height. "Thank you for informing us of the assassination plot, and for telling us the truth about why you left. Now if you'll excuse us, we have some plans to set in motion." He moved toward the door with his wife at his side, but then he paused. "Auric, would you join us?"

Auric nodded and left the room with one glance back at me. I swallowed the anxiety brimming inside me, hoping we'd done the right thing by telling his parents who we truly were.

20

JASIN

As we returned to our rooms that night, Kira touched my arm. "Jasin, are you all right?"

I glanced away. "Yes, why?"

"You were quiet during dinner. I don't think I've ever seen you get through a meal without making a joke or saying something a little inappropriate."

I lifted a shoulder. "Wasn't in the mood."

She took my hand and pulled me into her room, then shut the door. "Tell me the truth. What's bothering you?"

I sighed and sank onto the edge of her bed. "Auric's parents."

"What about them? You don't trust them?"

"No, nothing like that." I dropped my head, feeling foolish. "They're being so supportive and understanding even after Auric ran away, broke his engagement, and told them what he truly is."

She sat on the bed beside me and rubbed my back. "And you're remembering how your father turned us in to the Onyx Army."

"Something like that," I muttered. "Trust me, it would have been even worse if they'd known our goal was to overthrow the Dragons."

"I'm sorry. This must be difficult for you."

"I'm happy for Auric, but it's a bitter reminder that I'll never have a family like that. My parents always tried to mold me into something I'm not. They never supported what I wanted, and then they betrayed me. Now I'm not sure I'll ever see my parents again. If I'm honest, I'm not sure I want to either."

She wrapped her arms around me and rested her head on my shoulder. "You're right. Auric is a lucky man. My parents are gone, as are Reven's. Yours turned against you. And Slade's..." She paused. "I have no idea about his parents. But either way, you're wrong about the rest of it. You *do* have a family. You, me, and the other men—we're in this together for the rest of our lives."

I snorted. "The other guys? We barely get along."

"Isn't that common in all families?" She pressed her lips to my cheek. "One day maybe your parents will come around. But if not, please know that you'll always have us."

"All I need is you," I said, sliding my hand into her hair. I lowered my head and covered her mouth with mine, tasting her sweet, soft lips. My tongue slid across hers as her breasts pressed against my chest, her fingers digging into my arms. Through our bond I felt her desire flare bright, and I wondered if she sensed how much I wanted her too. No, not wanted. *Needed.* Ever since being chosen by the Fire God I'd been burning up inside, and Kira's touch was the one thing that sated me.

I tilted her head back and left a trail of kisses from her jaw to her neck to her collar. She wore that tempting green gown she'd gotten from Brin, and I slid the straps off her shoulder one at a time. The silken fabric slipped down her skin and pooled at her waist, revealing full breasts and nipples already hard for me. I cupped them in my hand while kissing along her shoulder, enjoying the way they filled up my palm, her skin cool against mine.

A knock sounded on the door and Kira lazily lifted her head. "Who is it?"

"It's me," Auric said.

"Come in," she called out.

Auric strode into the room. "Kira, I—Oh! Jasin... I'm sorry. I'll just go."

"It's okay," she said, beckoning him over. "What is it?"

As he walked inside, I continued trailing kisses down Kira's chest, then took a plump breast in my mouth. Auric cleared his throat as he moved close to the bed.

"I... I wanted to thank you for agreeing to tell my parents. It's good to have everything out in the open now." His voice sounded strained, and I imagined he was getting hard watching everything I was doing to Kira and the way she responded to me.

"I'm glad it all worked out," she said, before I flicked my tongue over her nipple and she let out a groan.

"Is it okay if I...watch?" Auric asked. "I'd like to see what Jasin does to please you as part of my training. But if that isn't okay anymore, I understand..."

"Stay," Kira said, her voice breathy and sensual.

Auric moved to the edge of the bed and watched as I continued worshipping her breasts with my mouth, while she buried her fingers in my hair. She reached for Auric and he knelt on the bed beside her, then she pulled his lips to hers. It seemed she wanted him to do more than just watch.

But then he broke off the kiss and sat back to watch again. I gestured for him to join me, and then circled one of Kira's hard nipples with the tip of my tongue. She let out a breathy moan that only grew louder when Auric copied me on her other breast. When I sucked her nipple, he did the same. Together we had her moaning our names as we lavished attention on her breasts until I sensed it was time to continue Auric's education in other ways.

"Lie back," I told Kira. As she followed my order, I dragged her gown down her body and off of her, admiring her shapely hips and legs while pressing a few light kisses to them. Auric stared at her naked flesh like he had never seen anything more beautiful, and I couldn't disagree.

I ran my hands along Kira's thighs as I spread her legs wide for me and kneeled between them. She was so responsive and so trusting, I had no doubt she'd let me do anything to her. The thought made me even harder than I already was, and I couldn't wait to be inside her, but I couldn't forget I'd agreed to teach Auric too.

As he moved to stand at my shoulder to get a better look,

I slid a finger between her folds. "Look how wet she is," I said.

"So beautiful," he whispered.

Kira moved her hands to cover herself, her pinks cheek. "You're making me blush."

I brushed her hands away. "Don't be embarrassed. We both think you're gorgeous. Now lie back and relax while I show Auric how to please you."

She rested her hands on either side of her and stared at the ceiling, while I took Auric's hand and brought it between her thighs. She let out a little gasp at the first touch of his fingers.

"Oh, Gods," he said, as I slid them slightly inside her, coating them in her wetness.

I released his hand. "Taste it."

Auric slowly licked the moisture off his fingers, while Kira and I watched. I didn't know why this turned me on so much, but it did. And I was pretty sure Kira felt the same.

"Like that?" I asked.

"Very much," he said.

"Good, because you're going to be tasting her a lot tonight." I took his hand again and dragged his fingers above her folds. As I found the right spot and had him start rubbing it, Kira began to moan again. "Feel that?" I asked, and Auric nodded. "That's the spot on a woman that brings them the most pleasure. If you forget everything else I'll teach you, remember that and you'll be fine."

Auric continued rubbing Kira there with a sly grin. "Ah yes, I've read about the clitoris in books."

I rolled my eyes. "Forget your books. Now watch and learn."

I shoved his hand aside and lowered my head between her thighs to finally taste her. I'd gone down on her once before at the Air Temple, but I'd never get enough of her sweetness or the sounds she made when my tongue flicked along her sensitive skin.

I showed Auric what I was doing with my mouth, and then grabbed his hand once more and slid his fingers inside of her. He got the hint and began pumping in and out in time to my tongue's movements on her clit, while he watched me intently. I had no doubt he was taking mental notes of everything I did along with Kira's response to it, even while he brought her pleasure at the same time.

It wasn't long before Kira was tightening her fingers on my hair and gripping Auric's arm while she came with a shout. I felt her tremble underneath me and had no doubt she was clenching up around Auric's fingers as well.

I sat back and grinned at him. "Nice work."

"That was incredible," he said. "I could feel her orgasm."

"Just wait 'til you're inside her at the time." I quickly removed my clothing, then moved up Kira's body and pressed my lips to hers, my cock nudging between her thighs. She kissed me back eagerly, wrapping one arm around my neck while reaching for Auric with the other.

"Did you like that?" I asked, as I dragged myself between her folds. "Both of us touching you at once?"

"Gods, yes." She whimpered a little as she lifted her hips. "Please, Jasin."

How could I deny her? I couldn't, and with a slight nudge I pushed inside her tight entrance. She moaned, but it was clear she wanted Auric involved too, even if they weren't ready for sex yet. With one smooth movement I rolled us over on the bed, so that she was on top of me. "Sit up."

She rose up on my lap, taking me even deeper while giving me a view of her breasts dangling in front of me. "Ohh," she said, as she closed her eyes and began to rock back and forth on me.

"That's it, ride me," I said, as I gripped her hips. "Auric, move behind her and touch her breasts."

He followed my command, and I had to admit I liked being the leader here in the bedroom. Kira leaned back into his touch as his hands covered her breasts and his mouth pressed against her neck. I rocked my hips up at her, slamming my cock deeper inside her, increasing our pace.

"Now touch her in that spot I showed you," I told Auric.

He reached down and slipped a hand between us to begin rubbing her clit. Kira threw her head back as she rode me faster, and I knew she was unable to stop as the pleasure built inside her. Auric still had one hand on Kira's breast, and I reached up to stroke the other one, while lifting my hips in time to her movements.

"That's it," I said. "Find your release."

She pressed her hands against my chest as she let out a loud moan and began to shudder, her body tightening up around me. Watching her face as she came was the most beautiful sight I'd ever seen, and I couldn't help but follow her over the edge as the pleasure crested inside me. But I kept lifting my hips and Auric kept rubbing her until every last bit of pleasure was teased from her body, when she finally collapsed against my chest.

Auric moved beside me and wrapped his arm around Kira, as she pressed a kiss to his lips and then mine. "Well, I'd say that first lesson was a success."

21

KIRA

When I'd imagined stopping in Stormhaven on our way to the Air Temple, I'd never pictured myself stepping into one of the finest dress shops in the city. Nor that Auric's fiancé would be the one who'd convinced me to come here.

"Lady Brin," the clothier said cheerfully as he made his way over to us and dropped into a bow. "It's wonderful to see you again."

Brin took his hands with a sweet smile. "Thank you, Dumond. How are your husbands?"

The elderly clothier's face crinkled as he beamed at her. "Quite well, thank you. What brings you to my shop today? Is there something I can get you?"

"You may have heard that Prince Auric has returned to the palace and a ball is being thrown in his honor tomorrow night. I plan to wear the lovely lavender gown you made me the other week, but my friend Kira needs something to wear too. I'm hoping you have something that would work for her."

"I see." His eyes flicked up and down me, like he was taking measurements. I wore another borrowed dress from Brin today, this one in a pale yellow. "I do believe I might have a few gowns that would do."

"Thank you," Brin said. "I'm sorry for the short notice."

He waved it away. "It's no trouble. That's why I always have a few gowns in stock at all times."

"And that's why you're the best."

"Let me see what I can find," he said, before slipping into the back room.

Brin and I casually admired the samples on the floor and touched the fabrics on display. Every gown in here was worth more than all of my life's possessions combined. I was keenly aware that I didn't belong in this fine shop full of brocades, silks, velvets, and jewels.

"I'm so glad you agreed to come with me," Brin said, as she idly examined a pair of soft deerskin gloves. "I realize we were both put in an awkward position due to the way we met, but I do hope we can become friends nevertheless."

"Friends?" I asked, startled.

"Yes. I have so few real friends. Auric is the only person I'm close to. The other nobles are always playing games with each other or are far too stuffy. And the rest...well, I tend to break their hearts." She winked at me. "Luckily that isn't an issue with you, since you already have four suitors."

I wasn't sure how I felt about being friends with my

mate's former fiancé, but I had to admit I found myself liking Brin despite myself. Instead of answering her, I asked, "Is there anyone you want to be with now that your betrothal with Auric has ended?"

"No one in particular. My family is trying to set up another marriage as soon as possible though." She sighed as she admired a deep green traveling cloak I'd been looking at earlier. "This would be lovely on you. I'll tell Dumond to add it to the order."

The clock cost more money than I'd ever had in my life. "But I can't—"

She held up a graceful dark hand. "No arguments, please. I have no sisters either, you know. It's nice to shop for someone other than myself. And Auric told me to get you whatever you wanted."

I wanted to protest some more, but the truth was I did need some new clothes, especially if we were going to be in Stormhaven for a few more days. I bowed my head. "That's kind of you both. Thank you."

"As the Prince's new betrothed, you'll have to start looking the part." When I made a face, she laughed. "Is that not so?"

"I suppose I am, though we've never talked about marriage. Our relationship is...complicated. And I'm still upset with him for not telling me about his betrothal to you."

"I saw him slip into your room last night, so you can't be that upset with him," she said, with a knowing gleam in her eyes.

My cheeks flushed at the memory of being touched by

Jasin and Auric together. "I've forgiven him somewhat, but not completely."

"You must understand that Auric has always been the odd one out among his family. They all love him, of course, but he's always kept to himself and been very independent. When he didn't, he was often teased by his siblings or ridiculed for being different by other nobles." She laid a hand on my arm. "When Auric neglects to tell you something, it isn't because he is trying to keep secrets, but because he has a hard time sharing parts of himself he knows others might disapprove of or dislike."

I sighed. "That doesn't excuse what he did."

"No, it doesn't, but I hope it explains it better." Her red lips quirked up. "But if you'd like, we can be mad at him together. I'm still upset he disappeared from the Air Realm without a word to me."

"He had a good reason, I promise."

She arched a perfect dark eyebrow. "Yes, though he still won't tell me what that is."

I was saved from having to answer when Dumond returned with two women who carried a gown each. "I believe either of these should fit with minimal alterations," he said. "Shall we try them on?"

I stepped behind a changing screen and donned the first dress, which was pale blue and made of the softest, lightest silk. It hugged my body when I put it on, accentuating my curves, and dipped scandalously low in the back. In the Air Realm people tended to show a lot more skin than I was used to, although I had to admit it did look nice.

I stepped out from behind the screen and Brin clasped her hands together. "Gorgeous," she said. "It fits you like a glove. Dumond, you are a genius."

He smiled at us both. "It helps when I have such beautiful women to work with."

I tried on the other gown next, which was pure white and covered in tiny clear crystals all over, with a low neckline and a skirt that slightly flared around my feet. I could only stare at myself in the mirror as I spun, the crystals shifting in color as they caught the light. My red hair hanging around my shoulders only added to the drama, as if the color had been heightened by the dress. My hazel eyes stood out too, like they were reflecting all the colors the dress caught.

Brin gasped when she saw me. "Oh, it's incredible. You must wear this to the ball."

I smoothed my hands down the skirts. "I've never worn something so fine in my life."

"Do you like it?"

In this gown I looked like a princess, like the kind of girl who belonged with Auric in the palace. "Yes, I love it. I'm just not sure I should be the one wearing it."

"Nonsense. We'll take both gowns," Brin told Dumond. "Although she'll wear this one to the ball."

He nodded. "Perfect. Let me make a few slight alterations and then we'll send them to the palace."

As he began sticking the dress with pins, I said, "Everyone is going to notice me in this dress."

"Good," Brin said. "You have the love of a prince. Why hide it?"

I couldn't help but smile. "I suppose."

While Dumond continued tacking the dress, Brin began picking out other things for me, such as shoes, jewelry, and accessories, plus that green cloak I'd liked. I decided to leave her to it, since I had no idea what would be proper for the ball and I could tell she loved doing this sort of thing.

Once I'd returned to my borrowed yellow gown and thanked Dumond for everything, Brin didn't stop there. She dragged me down the boisterous, colorful street to another shop, where I found fine traveling clothes that were more my style. The shopkeeper here knew Brin as well, and together they began picking out things for me.

By the time we were finished, I'd somehow ended up with an entire new wardrobe, courtesy of Brin's help and Auric's money. Every time I'd protested it was too much, Brin had ignored me. Now I had new boots, gloves, and riding clothes, along with my two gowns, two pairs of dress slippers, and much more. She even got me a few new chemises made of lace and silk, which I knew the men would love.

Hours later we climbed back into our carriage and relaxed against the seats. Who knew shopping could be exhausting? Or so time consuming? And the oddest thing was, I'd had fun, mainly because of Brin.

As the carriage began to climb the hill to the palace we both fell into tired, companionable silence while staring out the window. I'd been so hurt by Auric that I'd only thought of myself, but now I tried to imagine this situation from Brin's perspective. Her friend and betrothed had suddenly disappeared without a word and then returned over a month later with a new woman he loved and no explanation for where he'd been. Even if she didn't love Auric in that way it had to be difficult for her, especially with her family's pressure on her to marry. Yet she'd been nothing but kind to me.

"You should tell your parents you don't want them to arrange another marriage for you," I blurted out.

She blinked at my sudden words. "Why is that?"

"You deserve to be with someone you love. A marriage you don't want will never make you happy."

"You're probably right. At least if I married Auric I would be spending my life with a dear friend, but now my parents will likely try to marry me to someone I can barely tolerate. I do want children to further the family line someday, but I don't care for men in that way. But what choice do I have?"

It was hard to believe the confident Brin would balk at sticking up for herself, but things were always harder with one's own family. "What would you tell someone else who was in your position?"

She tilted her head slightly as she considered. "To be honest with their parents and be firm about what they want."

"Then that's what you should do."

A faint smile crept over her red lips. "It's much easier to give someone advice than to take it. Especially when it comes to standing up to your parents. But I'll try." She leaned forward and took my hands in hers. "Thank you, Kira. I can see why Auric loves you."

"And I can see why you're his best friend."

I hated to admit it, but we might be in danger of becoming friends too.

22

KIRA

When we returned from shopping, Brin slipped back to her rooms, but I stopped when I saw some familiar horses outside the palace—along with some familiar faces as well. Calla, the High Priestess of the Fire Temple, was dismounting, along with her four handsome mates. I rushed toward them and called out, "You're here!"

Calla smiled at me as she tucked back her pale blond hair. "Hello, Kira. I'm glad to see you're doing well."

"I'm so relieved you're all safe," I said. "Thank you for bringing the horses. How did you know we'd be here?"

"We knew you were heading to the Air Temple and assumed you would stop here first. Word spread that the King's youngest son had returned to the palace, so I thought I would leave the horses here for safe keeping. Although I presumed you would already be on your way to the Temple by now."

"We're leaving in two days." I sighed at the reminder. "I wanted to leave sooner, but there have been some...complications."

Calla nodded. "When you get to the Air Temple, please say hello to the High Priestess Nabi for me. She and I have corresponded many times, though we've never met in person."

"I will. But what are you all doing here and not at your own Temple?" I remembered Sark flying over the Fire Temple as we left. "Are you fleeing Sark?"

"Not exactly. He questioned us extensively for information on who you are and where you're going next, but I refused to tell him anything. We decided it wasn't safe at the Temple anymore after that."

I shuddered at the thought of facing Sark. "I'm so glad he didn't hurt you."

"Oh, he wouldn't dare. You see, Sark is my grandfather."

"Your *what*?" I tried not to cringe back in horror.

She chuckled softly. "That was my reaction too when I found out."

"I'm sorry," I said, my head spinning from the news. "I'm just surprised Sark let your relation stop him. He's always seemed so heartless and cruel."

"Yes, he is. But he's never hurt me or my mates, despite his threats over the years. He's never let the other Dragons harm us either. Perhaps it's a sign there's still some humanity left in him after all."

"I doubt that," I muttered. "I didn't even know the Dragons could have children."

"It seems they can, though I've never heard of any others like me, and I don't believe the Black Dragon can have any herself."

I'd never even considered children, though I should have when I'd slept with Jasin. The Black Dragon had ruled for hundreds of years with no children born to her, so in the back of my mind I must have known I could not become pregnant. Now that it was confirmed, a heavy sadness settled over me. Having a child wasn't something I'd thought about much growing up and living on the run, but after meeting my four mates, I couldn't help but wonder what it would be like to have children with each of them. Not anytime soon, but after we'd completed the momentous tasks ahead of us and our lives had calmed down. Would we never get that chance?

It mattered little, since I had more immediate problems to focus on. Sark knew about our existence, and even if he didn't know who we were or where we were going, it was only a matter of time before he was able to track us down.

After I bid Calla farewell and told her where she could find their boat, I sought out Auric, who was in the library with his head in a large, ancient-looking book, while a map was spread out beside him.

"Calla has arrived with our horses," I said.

He let out a relieved sigh. "Thank the Gods she is safe."

"She didn't tell Sark anything about us, but it won't be long before he realizes where we are. Are we still planning to leave for the Air Temple the morning after the ball?"

He tapped his fingers on the book idly. "Yes. I've been

making preparations, but I think we should ask Brin if she will go with us."

"Brin?" I shook my head. "I'm not sure that's such a good idea."

"We can trust her with the truth and we could use her help. No one knows the route to the Air Temple better than Brin."

"We agreed not to tell anyone after what happened with Jasin's family."

"Yes, but then we told my parents."

"That was different."

He gestured to the map. "The Air Temple is in the middle of the desert and it's easy to get lost out there without a guide, even with the best maps. I've only been once, but Brin's family goes every year. If we want to get there as quickly as possible, we need her guidance."

I stared at the map, then sighed. "All right, but we can't tell her what we are or why we're going to the Air Temple."

We called for Brin to join us, while a servant brought us all some tea and pastries. A few minutes later Brin sauntered into the library like it was her second home and smiled at us as she took a seat. "Hello again, lovelies. I was told you wanted to see me?"

Auric nodded. "We have something we'd like to talk to you about."

Brin's eyes sparkled as she leaned forward. "Are you finally going to tell me where you've been the last few weeks?"

"Not exactly." Auric cleared his throat and glanced at

me. "I'm sorry. I wish I didn't have to keep it a secret from you."

"It's all right," she said with a sigh. "What did you want to talk about?"

"We need to go to the Air Temple," I said. "And get there as quickly as possible."

Her eyebrows shot up and I could see her trying to put the pieces together. "Is that so? In that case, you'll need a lot of supplies, along with camels."

"Camels?" I asked.

"Of course. The Air Temple is surrounded by harsh desert with nothing around it for miles. Horses would have a difficult time there." She reached for a quill and some paper and began jotting things down. "You'll need lots of water, for sure, along with shelter capable of surviving the heat and sandstorms..."

"How do you know so much about this?" I asked.

"My family's ancestral home is on the edge of the desert, so I'm quite familiar with what it's like traveling there. I've also been to the Air Temple once a year for my entire life. My parents are quite devout." She scribbled across the paper, biting her lip. "Don't worry. I'll make sure you have everything you need."

"Thank you, Brin," Auric said. "I knew we could count on you."

"Of course, it's the least I can do for my dear friends."

"Would you possibly be interested in coming with us as our guide?" I asked.

She pressed a hand to her chest. "Oh, I would love to,

and I'm honored you've asked, but I can't. My parents want me to stay in Stormhaven to meet with potential suitors in the next few weeks. But don't worry, I'll make you an excellent map with the quickest route. I've done the trip in four days once, though much depends on the weather."

"That would be most appreciated," Auric said. "Thank you."

They began going over everything we would need, while I sat back and listened. In two days' time we'd be leaving Stormhaven behind and venturing into the desert. But could we make it to the Air Temple before the Dragons found us?

23

SLADE

On the day of the ball the palace descended into chaos. I managed to stay in my room for most of it, even though I found myself antsy and itching to be outdoors. I'd spent the past few days walking the palace grounds, trying to find some solitude with the earth and visiting the palace's blacksmiths to remind myself of who I was. Not a prince. Not an assassin. And not a soldier either. I was an ordinary man, and all I'd wanted was a simple life in my village. Now my life was anything but simple or ordinary.

I left to head out for a short walk outside to ground myself before the ball, but nearly ran into Kira in the hallway. She looked frazzled, wearing a white sparkling gown that was impossible to take my eyes off of, especially as it showed off every beautiful curve.

"Kira, what's wrong?" I asked.

She pressed a hand to her head and groaned. "My maid has disappeared and I need to finish getting ready for the ball and my hair is a mess and I have no idea what I'm doing. What will Auric's parents think of me when I show up like this?"

"You look beautiful." I took her arm and led her back to her room. "But let's see what we can do about your hair."

She followed me with a confused expression, but I sensed she was too frustrated at this point to argue with me. I knew she didn't feel like she belonged here, which was understandable. None of us did, not even Auric. But she wanted his parents to like her too, which I could also understand.

"Sit," I said, lightly pushing her into the chair at the dresser.

She sank down and stared at me in the mirror. "What are you going to do?"

I stood behind her and examined her for a moment, before picking up a brush. "I'm not sure yet."

I began to slowly run the brush through her glorious red locks, which shined with every stroke. Kira's hair was thick and had a tendency to get tangled, but I was gentle with it as I eased out the knots and pulled the brush through. She let out a soft sigh and her entire body relaxed under my care, though I suspected I might be enjoying it as much as she was.

I set down the brush and considered for a moment, then took small pieces of her hair in the front and began to braid it. She watched as I did this to both sides of her head before asking, "Where did you learn to do this?"

"From my sisters."

"You have sisters?"

I grunted. "Two of them. Both younger than me."

She smiled as I piled the rest of her hair atop her head and pinned it in an elaborate up-do with a few tendrils hanging down. "What are they like?"

"The younger one is a troublemaker. She's about your age and always finding ways to drive our mother mad, but she can put a smile on everyone's face she meets." I couldn't help but smile myself as I said it. "The other one is the quieter, more serious one. She married a few years ago and has a son."

"And your parents?"

"My father passed away some time ago from illness. My mother still lives, but hasn't remarried."

"I'm sorry."

I shrugged as I wrapped the braids around the bun I'd created. "It happened many years ago. I took over as village blacksmith, as was customary. Although now that I'm gone my cousin is running the shop."

"Do you miss your home?"

"Every day."

"I'd like to see it someday and meet your family too. Maybe on the way to the Earth Temple?"

"Maybe." I wasn't sure I wanted Kira to meet my family. That felt too...serious. I cleared my throat. "There. Finished."

"It's lovely. You're very talented at this." She admired her hair in the mirror with a smile. "Thank you."

"You're welcome."

She stood up and turned around, then wrapped me in a close embrace. "I know you didn't choose this and don't really want to be here, but I'm so happy you're one of my mates."

I couldn't help but hold her against me, drawn to her soft curves and feminine body despite myself, even as her words warmed me from the inside out. "No, I didn't choose this life, and I'm still not sure I'm the right man for the role, but I do want to be here."

She looked up at me with hope shining in her eyes. "You do?"

"Yes. I'm honored to be your Jade Dragon." I pressed a kiss to her forehead before releasing her. "And I think you'll be an excellent Black Dragon."

She sighed as she turned to admire her hair in the mirror again, touching it lightly. "I'm not sure I agree. The other day I was training with Jasin and couldn't control my magic." A small shudder passed through her. "What if I can never master it? What if I hurt someone by accident?"

I rubbed her shoulders as I met her eyes in the mirror. "You will master it, in time. The four of us had a month to train before we met you, and we're still learning. You only need more practice with fire."

"But soon I'll have air to learn too, and then earth and water." She covered her face with her hands. "It just seems so overwhelming and impossible sometimes."

I sensed she meant more than just learning the magic, but everything else that came with being the Black Dragon. When we'd started our journey together we'd all still been in disbelief, but now the implications of our new roles were starting to set in. "You have a lot resting on your shoulders, it's true. But I have no doubt you'll rise to whatever challenge you'll face in the future."

"That's nice of you to say. I wish I could believe it."

"Believe it," I said. "You're smart, capable, kind, and strong. The world could not ask for a better woman as the Black Dragon."

Her eyes softened and she turned toward me. "Thank you."

I looked away, unnerved by the warmth in her gaze. "I'm only speaking the truth."

She rested her hand on my cheek and turned my face back to her, then pressed her lips to mine. Something rumbled inside me as her soft mouth opened for me, and emotions I'd tried to keep buried deep now burst to the surface. I found myself gripping her arms as I began to slowly kiss her back, unable to stop myself. It had been a long time since I'd kissed anyone and I wanted to take my time with it. I needed to savor every taste of her sweet lips and every touch of her soft tongue.

But then I realized what I was doing and abruptly pulled away, as every reason I'd had for keeping my distance from her came rushing back. I couldn't lose my heart again, not to Kira, not to anyone.

I stepped back, while her face filled with confusion. "No, I can't do this. I'm sorry."

"Slade—" she started to say, but I was already dashing out the door, wiping my mouth to try to remove the taste of her from my lips. Except I had a feeling I would never be able to forget that kiss...or stop wanting another one.

24

KIRA

I stepped into the ballroom and was immediately enchanted by the sights and sounds inside. Spinning gold and silver decorations hung from the ceiling and caught the candlelight from around the room, making the room seem magical. A group of musicians played in a corner, while guests in exquisite clothes danced across the floor. An entire wall had been reserved for food and drinks, the likes of which I'd never seen before. I headed there first to sample the tiny dishes laid out, although the massive dessert table was hard to ignore. I'd never seen such extravagance before in my life, and while I'd expected to hate the ball, I wasn't going to complain. Especially as I popped a meat pastry puff in my mouth and nearly died at the flavors exploding across my tongue. I followed it with some sort of brie and raspberry tart, which was equally amazing.

"Enjoying yourself?" Reven asked from the shadows, as I

filled my plate with every single dish on the table. He wore all black, as usual, but tonight his clothes were finer than normal and he'd ditched the hooded cloak.

"Yes. Have you tried these?" I asked, before biting into a tiny sausage wrapped in more pastry.

He eyed my full plate. "I had one or two."

"Don't judge me. After being on the road for so long it's a nice change to eat like this, and it's not like I had the best meals before I met you either." Food in some parts of the world was hard to come by, especially when the Dragons demanded so much from their people. Back in Stoneham I'd usually eaten a little of whatever I'd caught in the forest after Tash had fixed it up for me. I'd certainly never had anything like the food in the Air Realm before.

Reven took a sip of his red wine. "Don't get too comfortable. We're leaving in the morning."

"I won't, but even you can admit it's nice to be able to relax and enjoy ourselves for one night at least."

He lifted a shoulder in a casual shrug. "I suppose."

Jasin strolled over with a grin, wearing a fine navy blue coat that accentuated his broad shoulders and muscular frame. He offered his hand and asked, "Care to dance?"

"I'd like to, but I don't know any of the fancy dances these nobles are doing," I said.

"Me neither." He winked at me as he took my arm in his. "But we'll manage."

I shoved my plate at Reven, who grumbled as Jasin swept me onto the dance floor and into the crowd. The crystal-covered gown I'd bought with Brin shimmered around me, and many people stopped to look at the way it caught the light. Or maybe they were looking at me because they'd heard rumors the prince had broken his engagement because of me.

As Jasin took me in his arms, he said, "You look lovely."

"Thank you." I smiled up at him, admiring how the red highlights in his auburn haired seemed to dance under the torchlight. "You cleaned up nicely yourself."

He swept me across the floor and we managed to move together in time to the music. "It's strange to not wear my uniform at things like this, but I suppose that part of my life is over."

"Do you miss being in the army?"

"Not at all." He brushed his lips across my cheek. "I'm exactly where I'm meant to be."

"You seem so certain." I longed for that certainty. Lately all I had were doubts, it seemed. Take earlier, for example. Slade had finally let me get close to him, but after I'd kissed him, he'd ran away. Now I didn't even see him in the ballroom. Was he avoiding me again?

"Meeting the Fire God will do that to a man, I guess." He touched my chin lightly. "Don't forget, he gave you his blessing as well."

"True. Sometimes I still can't believe it happened."

"Believe it. And you have three more Gods to meet soon."

I nodded. Maybe once we reached the Air Temple I'd find some more clarity. There was still so much I didn't know, like who my true parents were and why I was the

Black Dragon. I prayed the Air God would tell me something useful.

When the song ended, Auric appeared at my side wearing white and gold, with his blond hair slicked back and his gray eyes shining bright. "May I steal her away?"

"I suppose it's your party," Jasin said with a smile, as he stepped back.

Auric clasped my hand in his, then settled his other one on my waist. "I've never seen a woman more beautiful than you tonight."

My face flushed and I looked down. "That's very kind of you to say."

"It's the truth. Every other woman in his is jealous. Look how they stare at you."

"Only because I'm dancing with you. Do you think they know...?"

"Know what?" he asked, as he led me across the dance floor with surer steps than Jasin. He was obviously quite experienced with this kind of dancing.

"That you ended your betrothal because of me?"

"Definitely. Gossip travels fast. But don't worry, I care not what anyone thinks, and Brin is doing fine too." He nodded in the direction of the drink table. I followed his gaze to find Brin standing there with wine in hand, speaking to three women who hung onto her every word. "She'll take at least one of them to her room tonight, I'm sure. Maybe all three."

I arched an eyebrow. "I thought you were supposed to stay virgins until marriage, as was custom for nobility?"

"She's never been with a man before. I suppose she considers that good enough for tradition."

"Would her parents ever let her marry a woman?"

"Perhaps, but they'd want her to marry a man too. They want an heir."

I sighed. "I like Brin. I didn't want to, but I do."

He grinned as he spun me around. "She has a way of sneaking up on you like that. At first you think she's another spoiled noblewoman, but then you discover she's so much more. And you haven't even seen her fight yet."

"She can fight?"

"All nobles can, to some degree. We're taught to defend ourselves from a young age. But I daresay she might be even better than me."

"It's kind of her to help us prepare for the journey to the Air Temple."

Auric nodded, but whatever he might have said next was cut off when a hush went over the crowd. People around us stopped dancing and turned toward the front of the room, then unexpectedly dropped into low bows. Auric's grip on my arm tightened.

As the wave of bowing reached us, I was able to see over the crowd at last. Two men gazed across the room with haughty, cruel expressions. One of them was Isen, the Golden Dragon, wearing black and gold silk. He had some nerve showing up here after he'd just ordered an assassination on the King.

But then I noticed the other man standing beside him. Tall, broad shouldered, with short blond hair so pale it was nearly white, he was the man who'd haunted my nightmares for years. The last few times I'd seen him were in his dragon form and from a distance, but now he was only a few feet away as a man. A mix of terror and rage battled for dominance inside me. I knew I'd have to face him at some point, but I hadn't expected it to be anytime soon. But here he was, towering over this ball as though he ruled here instead of the King.

Sark, the Dragon who had killed my parents.

25

REVEN

The key to being a good assassin was to remain calm at all times—and I was the best in the four Realms. I'd faced impossible odds and dodged certain death without breaking a sweat. I'd escaped prisons and survived torture. I'd stolen from the best thieves and murdered the most vile men and women. And never once had I lost my calm.

Until tonight.

The sight of Sark sent instant, poisonous hatred through my veins and I reached for my hidden weapons without thinking. With a small dagger in each hand, I charged forward—but was held back by a large hand on my shoulder.

"You don't want to do that," Slade said.

"Trust me, I do." I pulled away from him with some effort. Damn, the man was strong. It was like fighting against a boulder.

"Someday, yes. But not here. Not now. Not yet."

I gripped my daggers tighter, the rage boiling me from the inside out at the sight of the man standing there while people bowed before him. I wanted nothing more in the world than to stab my blade through his heart. Or better yet, make him suffer the way he'd made me suffer. The way he'd made Kira suffer.

But Slade had a point, though I was reluctant to admit it. If I stabbed Sark, would he even die? We knew so little about the Dragons since no one had dared oppose them. For all we knew they were immortal. They only way to defeat them was to become Dragons ourselves.

I sheathed my daggers and muttered, "Fine."

That didn't mean I would stand by doing nothing. I slipped back into the shadows, while Auric's parents made their way over to the uninvited guests with fake smiles plastered on their faces. I ducked behind statues and tables to get closer, but I wasn't planning on attacking, only listening. Although if the moment presented itself, I wouldn't mind attacking either.

"Sark, Isen, what an unexpected appearance," the King said.

"Are we not welcome?" Isen asked, arching a black eyebrow.

"Of course you are. We're delighted to have such esteemed guests. I'm simply surprised since you do not often grace our balls with your presence."

"Sark and I have business in the city and thought we might stop by." Isen cast a dismissive gaze across the crowd, which had reluctantly started dancing again, though the mood in the room had changed and become tense. "I heard there'd been an assassination attempt on your life. Is that so?"

"Yes, there was, but we dealt with it. The assassin is dead." The King paused. "You wouldn't know anything about that, would you?"

"You dare question us?" Sark asked, his voice more like a growl.

King Terel smiled at them like they were old friends. "Not at all. Simply hoping for some answers. But we'll uncover who was behind it, I'm certain."

Isen sniffed. "And that matter we discussed the other day? Have you had time to think on it?"

The King hesitated, then bowed his head. "Yes, I have, and I concede to your wishes. Tomorrow we'll begin searches throughout the city for Resistance members."

"See that you do," Isen said, his voice carrying a subtle threat. "Otherwise I can't promise there won't be more trouble in the Air Realm."

"We have reason to believe five people in particular are hiding in Stormhaven," Sark said. "One woman and four men. They might claim to have special powers, but they are tricksters and con artists. If you hear word of them, inform us immediately."

"I shall," King Terel said.

"Enjoy your party," Isen said, as he turned away and plucked a tiny pastry off the dessert table and popped it in his mouth. He gestured at Sark, but the Crimson Dragon stared at something behind the King, his brow furrowed.

I followed his gaze and saw Kira's pale face looking back at him. Auric held her in his arms, and I couldn't be sure if he was keeping her from running to attack Sark, like Slade had done with me, or if he was holding her up so her knees wouldn't give out on her. That burning hatred seethed inside me again as Sark took Kira in, and I reached for my daggers in case he recognized her somehow. But then Sark spun on his heel and followed Isen outside onto the patio, where it had begun raining. They both shifted into their dragon forms and took off, while lightning flashed in the sky and thunder rumbled behind it.

As soon as they were gone a collective sigh of relief went up around the entire room and the dancing picked up. Even the music seemed livelier and the candles brighter. The Dragons had a tendency to suck the air out of any room they were in. Was it any wonder I had no desire to become one of them?

But that was before. Now, as I caught sight of Kira's pained expression and trembling hands, a new purpose and resolve filled me. Sark had taken everything from Kira, just as he'd done to me. Even so, I hadn't wanted revenge, not at first. I'd made my own way in the world and found a way to survive. After I'd been appointed the next Azure Dragon I'd tried to run from my destiny, but I'd been unable to stay away.

Everyone I'd ever loved was dead. I refused to love Kira and have her meet the same fate, but for some reason I wasn't able to walk away from her either. Gods knew I'd tried, yet here I was, drawn by this invisible string to her side no matter how much I tried to fight it or escape it. Maybe, deep down, I'd known this was the only way to avenge my family and take down the beast responsible for their deaths. The best way to fight fire was with water, after all.

To defeat Sark, I had to become a Dragon myself. And this time, I wouldn't run or hide from my fate. I would be the next Azure Dragon, no matter what it took.

I just had to make sure I didn't lose my heart to Kira in the process.

26

KIRA

After Sark's arrival at the ball and the way he'd looked at me, like he'd recognized me somehow, I hadn't wanted to dance any longer. Fear and anger had taken hold of my heart, and all I could do was return to my room and take deep breaths to calm myself. I reminded myself if Sark truly had recognized me or realized what I was, I'd be dead now. We were still safe and our identities were unknown, though I knew that wouldn't last much longer.

The Dragons were looking for us, that was for sure. Thanks to Calla, they didn't know who we were or even what we looked like, but it was only a matter of time before we were uncovered. Good thing we were leaving for the Air Temple in the morning.

A massive storm had begun raging as soon as the Dragons had left, and I stared out my window as dozens of lightning bolts hit the spires across the city, filling the sky with dazzling light. Thunder rumbled all around us, as if the Air God himself was displeased.

Heavy footsteps sounded outside my door, which was then thrown open. All four of my mates stood in the doorway looking as if they were going to charge in here with their weapons drawn to defend my honor.

Jasin stood at the front of the group, his dark eyes blazing. "Kira, are you all right?"

"You disappeared from the ball without a word," Auric said.

I gave them a faint smile. "Yes, I'm fine. I was just a bit shaken from seeing Sark and needed to get away from the crowd."

"Everyone in the entire room was shaken," Reven said. "The Dragons do that to people."

Auric's hands clenched into fists. "They had some nerve coming to the ball uninvited and threatening my father in front of everyone."

"Your father handled it well," I said. "Better than I would have."

"He's had many years of practice. And you did well too."

"I didn't. If not for you, I would have done something embarrassing." I shuddered when I remembered Sark's terrible gaze. "I thought for sure he recognized me at the end."

"He didn't," Slade said. "Or we'd all be dead."

"I thought the same thing." I sighed as I sank down onto

the bed. "I wish I'd been able to face him without fear, but I was terrified. How am I supposed to actually fight the Dragons someday?"

Auric sat beside me and wrapped an arm around my shoulders. "You'll get there. No one expects you to fight them now. Or any of us for that matter. We have to unlock all of our powers first."

I leaned against him. "What if the Dragons stop us from getting to the temples?"

"We'll find a way somehow."

I nodded, but I wasn't convinced, and I couldn't get Sark's harsh voice out of my head. Nor Isen's cruel one, for that matter. At least the King had gone along with the plan to accede to some of their wishes to keep his family safe. I hoped we could count on his help someday too—we might need it.

"We have an early start ahead of us," Slade said. "Best we all get some rest."

The men agreed, but the thought of being alone in my room left a hollow pit in my stomach. I looked up at the four of them and asked, "Will you all stay with me tonight?" When they stared at me, I added, "Just sleep, nothing more. I just don't want to be alone, and I think I'll feel better if you're all by my side. But if you don't want to, that's fine also. I understand."

"You know I'm always happy to share your bed," Jasin said.

"Me too," Auric added.

Slade frowned and glanced at the bed. "Not sure it's big enough for all of us."

"Sure it is," Jasin said, as he flopped onto the bed. He patted the spot next to him. "We just have to get nice and cozy."

I laughed despite my dark mood and slid onto the bed beside him. He immediately wrapped me in his strong arms and pulled me close, pressing a kiss to my temple. Auric climbed onto the bed on the other side of me and draped his arm over my waist, caging me between the two of them, which was becoming one of my new favorite places to be. Slade reluctantly got onto the bed too beside Jasin, his body stiff as he kept his distance from us as much as possible. He'd likely get a sore neck and I wished he was touching me too, but at least he was here with me instead of pushing me away.

"I'll sleep in the chair, thanks," Reven said.

I reached for him, my heart aching with longing. "Reven..."

"That bed is plenty crowded without me joining in. Besides, someone should keep watch." He settled into a chair and propped his feet up on the table, crossing his arms behind his head.

I sighed, but I couldn't force him to want to be with me. He was in the room watching over me and that was enough, especially when he'd left me behind only a few days ago. The fact that he stayed now was a big step up.

"Thank you," I murmured, as I buried myself into Jasin

and Auric's warm bodies. I reached over and ran a hand along Slade's muscular arm too, taking comfort from his nearby presence. I even felt Reven's closeness and support as I closed my eyes and drifted away.

When I woke, I found the three of us tangled together, limbs entwined, my hair draped across them, our heartbeats all in sync. Even Slade had come closer during the night as if he couldn't resist, and now his hand rested on my hip, while my foot rested on his calf. Jasin and Auric were wrapped around me too, and I was blissfully warm and calm for the first time in ages.

Except I really had to relieve myself.

I managed to untangle myself from the men without waking them, though Jasin reached for me and mumbled for me to come back. Reven's eyes popped open as I padded across the floor to the washroom.

"Sleep well?" he asked, showing no sign he'd been asleep at all.

"Very." I rested a hand on his shoulder. "Though I wish you would have joined us too."

"I don't think that's ever going to happen. Even if I wanted to, the other guys don't want me there with you. They don't trust me. For good reason, I admit."

"They will. Just give them time." I bent down and brushed my lips across his dark, stubbled jaw, making his shoulders tense up. I wanted to do more, so much more, but I had to be sure he wanted that too.

I slipped away to the washroom, and when I returned all

the men were stretching and waking up, while morning light filtered through the curtains. Though I would have liked to return to bed with them, and possibly do more than sleep, it was time to get going. The Air Temple awaited us.

27
AURIC

We gathered outside the palace, where two carriages were waiting for us with our supplies already loaded onto them. The plan was to take the carriages out of the city and to Windholm, a town on the edge of Sandstorm Valley. There we would switch to camels for the rest of the journey into the barren desert where the Air Temple resided.

Brin and I had been overseeing preparations over the last two days, and I was grateful for her assistance since I hadn't been in the desert in many years and had never planned an excursion on my own. It was a shame she wouldn't be going with us, but it would be hard to hide what we were if she did come, so perhaps it was for the best.

My former fiancé stood with Kira by the carriages, while stroking the neck of a dappled gray horse. Kira laughed at something Brin said, and my heart warmed at the sight.

Against all odds they'd managed to become friends, just as I'd hoped.

Kira wore her new riding clothes with a dark green cloak that brought out the color in her eyes and made her red hair pop. She had new boots too, and I was pleased to see that her shopping excursion with Brin had gone well and that she'd been able to obtain some suitable clothes, which she'd desperately needed.

Her mates had been more stubborn and wouldn't accept my offer to get them new clothing, although they'd allowed me to loan them things to wear while we were at the palace. I'd ceded defeat, but had made up for it by providing all of the supplies we'd need on this journey. It was the least I could do for the trouble I'd put us in by coming here, and for their understanding of my situation with Brin.

While Kira's other mates checked our supplies, I turned to the ladies and asked, "Are we all ready to go?"

"Just about," Brin said. "We just need to say goodbye to your parents."

I arched an eyebrow at her. "We?"

"I've decided to come with you after all." Brin flashed a dazzling smile at us. "You're going to need a guide. And thanks to Kira here, I'm a free woman."

"What do you mean?" I asked.

"Kira convinced me to stand up to my parents and tell them I wouldn't go through with an arranged marriage to a man. They weren't thrilled about it, but they said they understood."

"I'm so proud of you," Kira said.

I wrapped Brin in a quick hug. "That's wonderful. And they're allowing you to go on this journey?"

She tossed back her long black hair with a grin. "The King convinced them it would be good for you to have an escort, though I'm pretty sure they think we're just going to offer tribute at the Air Temple. Not that I know what we'll actually be doing, but I have a feeling it's more than that."

"Are you sure about this?" Kira asked. "It's going to be dangerous. The Dragons are searching for us, and we've also been attacked by bandits, elementals, and the Onyx Army."

"Sounds like you need someone to help watch your backs," Brin said with a wink. "Believe me, I'm ready to get out of this boring city and see some adventure. My blades haven't been put to good use in ages."

"All right, but if it gets too dangerous we're leaving you at the Air Temple," I said.

Brin waved her hand breezily. "I'll be fine. Besides, we all know you'll need my help so you don't end up wandering in circles out in the sand dunes."

"We appreciate you coming with us," Kira said. "I've never been to the desert before."

"It's beautiful in its own way, but deadly. Although with proper preparations we should be fine."

Our conversation died off when my parents walked out of the palace, their guards trailing behind them. The King loomed over everyone as he made his way down the steps while holding my mother's arm. Both of them wore royal purple and gold along with their crowns as they came to say goodbye to us.

I approached my parents with a hesitant smile, while Brin and Kira trailed behind me. "Mother, father."

The King stared at me for some time, then clasped me on the shoulder. "We're proud of you, son."

I'd never heard those words from my father before and my throat choked with emotion. "Thank you," I managed to get out.

"Please be safe," my mother said, as she squeezed me in a tight hug. "And come back whenever you can."

"I will, and I'll send updates if it's safe to do so."

She nodded and turned to Kira, then surprised me by embracing her too. "I'm sorry we didn't have more time to get to know you better, but I hope we can do so someday."

"I'd like that," Kira said. "Thank you for your hospitality."

The Queen turned to Brin next and gave her a warm smile. "Brin, please take care of these two."

"I will, your majesty," Brin said, as she dipped into a graceful curtsy.

My father nodded at the two ladies, and then focused his stormy gaze on me once more. "Before you go, there's something we'd like you to have." He gestured at a servant, who walked up holding a purple tasseled pillow. On top of it were two long, slightly curved daggers with golden sheaths and hilts inlaid with topaz.

The King lifted the daggers in his palms. "These are the blades of the first King of the Air Realm, who was said to be the brother of the Golden Dragon. I'd once thought that meant Isen, but now I'm not so sure. Either way, they've been passed down through generations to our family's greatest warrior. And now, Auric, we want you to have them."

I accepted the blades with awe in my voice. "I'm honored. Thank you. I'll do my best to restore honor to the position of Golden Dragon."

"We know you will," my mother said, as she patted my cheek.

I strapped the daggers around my waist, noticing how light they were despite their size and their golden sheaths. I'd seen the daggers hanging in the royal armory before and was shocked my parents were giving them to me and not to my brother Garet, who was the warrior in the family. All my life I'd been the odd one out and I'd believed I was a disappointment to my parents. This was finally my chance to make them proud and do my duty to protect the Air Realm —and the entire world.

I said one final goodbye to my parents, before turning away with my heart pounding loudly. Kira gave me a warm smile, while Brin's eyes shined bright. Together we approached the carriages, where the other men were waiting.

I nodded at them. "Let's get going."

KIRA

I watched through the carriage window as we left the city, but then my eyes grew heavy and I found myself dozing off. I suspected the others were doing the same. Leaving early after a long night at the ball was probably not the best idea, but none of us had wanted to delay any longer, not with the Dragons sniffing around for us.

According to Brin, it would take us five days to reach the Air Temple with her guidance. Two of those days would be spent in carriages, which wasn't the worst way we'd traveled so far. The men grumbled and complained, saying they wished they were back on their own horses and out in the open air, especially with the stuffy heat inside the carriage. For me this was a treat since I'd never had my own horse and had always had to ride behind one of them. The boat wasn't so bad either, except for the cramped quarters, but least Slade wasn't sick to his stomach in the carriage.

As night fell, we entered the town of Skydale and were taken by our guards and drivers to the finest inn, since nothing less would befit the prince. I didn't think Auric cared, but while we were traveling as part of a royal caravan we had to keep up appearances. Once we reached Windholm tomorrow we would discreetly leave behind our entourage and make our way into the desert alone. The carriages and royal guard would continue on to Thundercrest to make it seem as though the prince was visiting his brother Garet.

After using the washroom, I returned to my room and found Jasin and Auric already inside, talking low to each other with grins on both of their faces. They sat on the edge of the bed like they were waiting for me.

"What are you two gossiping about?" I teased, though it warmed my heart to see them both getting along.

"We were discussing Auric's lesson tonight," Jasin said.

"Is that so?" I asked.

Auric nodded. "We're only a few days away from the Air Temple and I want to be ready."

Jasin gave me a naughty grin. "Auric is going to pleasure you with his mouth tonight. How does that sound?"

The thought sent a rush of heat between my thighs, but I had an idea too. "I wouldn't complain, but I want to learn to do that too."

Jasin arched an eyebrow. "Is that so?"

I slid the straps off my gown and let the silken fabric shimmer down to the floor, revealing my naked skin underneath. Both men's eyes dropped to take in every inch of me.

"I want to bring you pleasure with my mouth too, the way you do to me."

"Trust me, you already bring us pleasure," Jasin said. "But I'm always happy to teach you anything."

I moved close to him and he watched with hooded eyes as I opened his trousers slowly to reveal his large, hard shaft. I lifted his shirt up and off him next, then let my hands run along his muscular chest, enjoying the feel of him underneath my palms. He leaned back and let me touch him, and then I tugged his trousers off him, leaving him as naked as I was.

I wrapped my hand around Jasin's cock and he let out a groan. I'd had him inside me twice now, but had never touched him like this before. Now I wanted to get to know this part of him a lot better.

"Like this." Jasin wrapped his hand around mine and showed me how to stroke him the way he liked. I followed his movements until he released me and threw his head back, his eyes closed as he enjoyed my touch.

Auric watched with keen eyes the entire time from beside us, but he didn't join in. Last time he hadn't even removed his clothes, but tonight I wanted him to be more than just an observer. With one hand holding Jasin's cock, I reached for Auric and tried to tug off his shirt. He helped me get it off and then I ran my fingers along his hard nipples and down his long, muscular torso. When my hand reaches his trousers and began fumbling there, his eyes widened.

"Kira, are you sure?" he asked.

"Yes, I want you to join us tonight."

He kissed me hard in response, and I could taste the desire on his lips. My fingers yanked open his trousers, and I was greeted with his hard manhood. He was longer than Jasin, but not as thick. I wondered what it would be like to have him inside me, and if it would feel different than Jasin, as I wrapped my other hand around his cock.

Jasin and Auric both began touching me too, smoothing their hands across my skin as I stroked them together. They cupped my breasts and brought my nipples to their lips. They gripped my behind and yanked me closer against them. They let their fingers dip between my thighs to touch me in places that made me moan too.

But then Jasin pulled away. "Auric, lie back on the bed. It's time to start the next lesson."

Desire stirred inside me at his commanding tone. I had to admit I liked it when Jasin became dominant in bed. I think he enjoyed being the teacher more than he'd expected too.

When Auric was in position, I stared at his body with hunger, until Jasin said, "Kira, you're going to straddle his face. Don't worry, you won't hurt him."

I climbed up onto the bed and moved into position, while Auric's hands came up and began stroking my thighs and my bottom. With my legs spread wide and his face beneath me, I felt more exposed than ever, especially with Jasin watching intently from the side.

Auric gripped my thighs and lowered me to his mouth, and I let out a sigh as his tongue slid against me. He worked slowly, exploring and tasting every inch of me, until I was completely relaxed. Only then did Jasin move in front of me and kneel on the bed, his cock standing proudly at attention and making my mouth water.

Jasin slid his fingers into my hair as he kissed me roughly, then broke away and pushed my head down. I understood immediately and lowered my mouth to his shaft. At first I ran my tongue along it, tasting him and seeing what it did to him. But then his fingers gripped my hair tighter, and I opened my mouth to wrap around the tip of his cock.

"Yes, just like that," he said, as he slowly pushed deeper into my mouth. He took my hand and wrapped it around the base of his cock, while my other hand gripped his bottom for support.

Auric took this moment to slide two fingers inside me, while sucking and licking on me in that spot Jasin had showed him before. Pleasure unfurled inside me and I moaned around Jasin, who sank deeper between my lips in response. I stroked him and sucked on him, my hands and my mouth working in time, and his hips thrust against me in response. Even though his fingers in my hair kept me down I felt so powerful knowing I could bring him pleasure like this.

With Auric's mouth bringing me higher and higher and his fingers pumping inside me, I matched his movements around Jasin's cock. Suddenly it became too much and my thighs began to tremble. Jasin held me steady as pleasure consumed me and I moaned around him, while Auric kept licking and thrusting into me.

As the spasms faded, Jasin pulled out of my mouth and

gathered me in his arms to help me off of Auric, who sat up and wiped his mouth with a grin. "Gods, you taste good. I could do that forever."

"You've had your turn," Jasin said. "Now I need her."

He spun me around and gripped my hips, pulling my bottom up. Now on my hands and knees, he loomed behind me, his hands on my behind.

"Mm, you have a lovely ass." His fingers dipped between my thighs, getting nice and wet, but then he moved them back between my cheeks. "I wonder if you'd ever let one of us enter you here."

The thought had never occurred to me before, and my eyes widened as he slid a finger along my back entrance. I gasped as he pushed slightly inside and a new wave of pleasure moved through me.

"I think she likes the idea of that," Auric said.

"Yes, she does." Jasin lowered his voice as he moved his finger slowly in and out of my tight hole. "She wants both of us inside her at once. Not tonight. But soon."

I couldn't help but thrust my hips back against him at the delicious image of being filled by both men, and Jasin chuckled softly. "Please," I found myself begging.

Jasin gripped my hips, then suddenly entered me from behind in one smooth thrust that had me crying out. He felt huge from his angle, like every inch of him was filling up every inch of me. My fingers dug into the sheets as he began to move in and out of me, controlling my hips to get the best angle. All I could do was throw my head back and enjoy.

But I wanted to touch Auric too. He'd brought me pleasure both times, but had never asked for any in return. "Come here," I told him.

Auric kneeled in front of me, and I lowered my mouth to his long cock. "Oh, Gods," he groaned, as I circled his shaft with my tongue, before wrapping my lips around him. Unlike Jasin, who had guided my movements, Auric stroked my head lovingly while I sucked on him.

With both men inside me, they found a smooth rhythm that brought me nearly to the edge already. Jasin thrust forward, pushing me further onto Auric before retreating again. Between the heat and solidness of Jasin entering me from behind, and Auric's length and musty taste in my mouth, I knew I wouldn't last long.

Auric's fingers suddenly tightened in my hair, and his cock pulsed under my tongue. "Kira, I can't—Ohhh..."

I sucked him harder in response, growing more excited knowing I'd done this to him. Jasin slipped a hand between my thighs and began to rub me in time to our movements, and soon I was moaning too. That sent Auric over the edge, and he released himself in my mouth with one last thrust, shouting my name.

"Swallow it," Jasin commanded, and I did my best to comply.

As I licked Auric clean, Jasin pumped into me faster and harder, his grip on my hips tightening while his finger continued rubbing me too. I threw my head back and cried out loudly as my second orgasm struck me like a lightning bolt, and I felt Jasin join me in bliss only moments later.

Jasin gathered me in his arms as we collapsed onto the

bed together. Auric curled up behind me, and I snuggled back against him too.

Jasin slowly kissed me, then he reached over and gave Auric's arm a squeeze. "You were both amazing."

"We're fast learners," Auric said, grinning back at him. They were so comfortable with each other now, as if they had become bonded too in the process of sharing me.

I nuzzled closer against them both. "We had a good teacher."

29

SLADE

The walls of this inn were way too thin. Much worse than at the palace, where I'd only heard a few brief moans. Now I heard *everything*.

I tossed and turned, even put the pillow over my head, but nothing helped. In the other bed Reven seemed to be asleep, but who could tell with him. If he was awake he probably didn't care, since he seemed to have no feelings for Kira at all.

Eventually Kira and her two lovers quieted down, though it took forever. But even then, sleep was elusive. I couldn't stop picturing her with both Jasin and Auric, torn between wishing I was with her too and wanting her for myself alone. I replayed our kiss in my head a dozen times, but all it did was make me frustrated. With myself, with the situation, with the other guys for being with her tonight. Somehow I had to get a grip on myself and my emotions.

In the morning, we got back in the carriages and continued on through the Air Realm, where the landscape started to become sparse with trees and the ground became rockier. I hated being in the carriage almost as much as being in the boat, and it didn't help that I was stuck with Jasin and Kira either. Every time they touched or giggled like lovers my teeth clenched and I glared out the window.

"Are you all right?" Kira asked me. "You seem...tense."

"Didn't sleep well," I said.

"I know a good cure for that," Jasin said with a sly grin. "Maybe we should invite Slade to our next 'lesson.'"

I crossed my arms. "Not interested."

Except I was, just a tiny bit. It was curiosity and nothing more, I told myself. We didn't share lovers in the Earth Realm, and I couldn't imagine doing it now either, even if the thought did rouse some lust within me. Probably because it had been many years since I'd been with a woman. I tamped those feelings down since I would never act on them. The others could have their fun, but my plan was to bond with Kira at the Earth Temple and that was it.

When we stopped at midday to relieve ourselves and have a bite to eat, I practically launched myself out of the carriage and away from Jasin and Kira.

Kira started to follow me and called out my name, but I kept going until I'd found a bit of privacy behind some bushes and a group of olive trees. All I needed was to be alone with the ground under my feet and then I'd feel better.

Footsteps padding in the dirt told me my solitude wasn't

going to last. Kira stepped into the shade under the trees with me. "There you are."

"Just needed some space after being in that carriage all day."

"I can understand that, but you've been distant for a while now." She reached out to brush her fingers against my hand. "Is something bothering you?"

"No, I..." I stared down at the spot where we were touching. "It's nothing."

"You can tell me anything, Slade."

I scowled and ran a hand along my beard, choosing my words carefully. "I know sharing partners is common in some parts of the world, and in our situation it's unavoidable, but it's hard for me to accept. When a woman is mine, I want her to be all mine."

She swallowed, her eyes widening with what I thought might be desire, though that made no sense. "I'm still getting used to the idea of having four lovers too. I'm sorry it bothers you though."

"Ignore me," I said, shaking my head. "I'll do my duty, just as you will."

Her face fell. "Is that all I am to you? A duty?"

"Not at all. I care for you a great deal, Kira. I will protect you until my dying breath. And when the time comes, I will bond with you. But please do not ask me for anything more than that."

"I don't understand. The other night we kissed and I thought..." She sighed. "I do want to be yours, Slade. And I want you to be mine too."

Longing stirred within me, along with the desire to haul her into my arms and kiss her again. I wanted nothing more than those soft, sweet lips on mine and her supple body pressed against me. But giving in to those desires would only make this more complicated. I couldn't get hurt again the way I'd been hurt before. The best thing to do was to end any pretense that we would become romantically involved. She had the other men, and that would have to be enough.

I stepped back out of her reach. "I'm sorry, Kira. I'll give you my body and my soul, but I can never give you my heart."

As I headed back toward the carriage, I told myself it was for the best, even if I hated leaving her there like that. She deserved better, but I was the one the Earth God had chosen, and we'd both have to find a way to live with that.

3 0

KIRA

When we returned to the carriages Slade made sure to be in a different one than me, and my heart sank even further. Every time I saw him I wanted him to wrap me in his strong arms and hold me close—or push me down and have his way with me. After our kiss the other night those thoughts were stronger than ever, but he'd made it clear he didn't see me in that way.

My four mates had been chosen by the gods to be mine, and in the process they'd had to give up their former lives to go on this quest with me. Only Auric and Jasin had been happy about that so far, while Reven and Slade had fought against their new roles. Though they'd both accepted their position now, I wasn't sure if they would ever love me or truly want to be with me.

I had two incredible men who wanted me—wasn't that enough? Except when I thought of Slade or Reven my chest clenched and I knew it wasn't. How selfish was I that I wanted all of my mates to love me?

While the sun was setting we arrived in Windholm, a small, dusty town with tumbleweeds rolling through it. Here the pace was a lot slower than in Stormhaven, and the people wore cloaks and scarves to cover their faces to protect against the frequent sandstorms. We were taken to another inn and retreated to our rooms, while Brin sorted out the details in town. And then we waited.

I managed to sleep a little, but woke instantly when Auric touched my arm and said, "It's time."

Brin presented me with a stack of clothes. "Put these on."

I donned a large, sand-colored cloak over my clothes, then pulled the hood low while yanking the scarf up so that only my eyes were visible. The others in our group did the same, and then we slipped from the inn and out into the dark, empty streets. A raging wind was already rolling through the town, and I ducked my head and followed Brin around the side of the inn, where a few people were waiting with camels. None of them gave us a second glance and no one seemed to recognize Auric. Not only did the cloaks protect us from the winds, but they disguised us as well.

I'd never ridden a camel before, but nevertheless was pleased to have my own mount this time. All of the beasts were sitting on the ground, and a man instructed me to throw my leg over the middle of the humps to mount the camel nearest me. The beast began to stand immediately, back legs first, making me fall forward, but I managed to find my balance after a moment.

Our supplies were already tied onto the camels, and then Brin took the lead. "Don't bother trying to control your camel. Just relax, let your body follow its movements, and try not to upset them. They're not particularly friendly."

With that warning she set off, and my camel jerked forward after hers. I had to hold on tight to keep from falling off as the beast's body rolled with an odd, jerky walk, completely different from the measured gait of a horse. At first my body wanted to fight it, but then I tried to relax my shoulders and follow Brin's advice, and it became much easier as I swayed with the camel's movements.

Soon we were riding out of town and down the hard dirt road into the desert at the bottom of the hill. The contrast was sharp and came upon us quickly, and in no time our camels' hooves were dipping into the sand. The mountains rose up on either side of us, the wind howled loudly, and the barren desert of Sandstorm Valley stretched endlessly before us.

We rode in a line through the sand for hours while the sun rose in the sky and beat down on us. Sweat dripped down my forehead, and I quickly became disoriented as we passed over identical dune after dune. All I saw around us was sand, which the wind kicked up into our eyes.

Brin called for a halt when the sun had neared its peak in the sky. We set up camp with small tents that would protect us from the worst of the sun and heat, and the men subtly used their magic to help us without alerting Brin.

Reven refilled all of our water jugs, Jasin roasted a lizard he'd caught and ate it off a stick, and Auric and Slade kept the wind and sand out of our camp.

I wandered down a dune to find some privacy to relieve myself and to have a moment alone with my thoughts. The closer we got to the Air Temple the more apprehensive I became. Was I ready to bond with Auric? Would the Dragons be there waiting? And what was I going to do about Slade and Reven?

As I climbed down the dune, the sand slid under my feet, endlessly changing. Just when I'd think I'd found a firm bit to walk on it would shift and my foot would sink, making me stumble.

"Careful there," a familiar voice said.

I spun around and came face to face with Enva, the older woman I'd met twice before. She'd always appeared out of nowhere and would disappear just as quickly, leaving me with more questions than answers. I'd once wondered if she was the Spirit Goddess, but she'd claimed she wasn't. "Enva, what are you doing here?"

Unlike me, she wasn't dressed for the desert. In fact, she wore the same hooded robe she'd worn the last two times I'd seen her. "Keeping an eye on you. I thought you'd be at the Air Temple by now."

"Why do you care so much about my fate?" I asked.

She waved my question away. "I care about the fate of the world, as should everyone."

I plopped down onto the sand, exhausted after hours of riding under the hot sun. My tailbone winced in protest, sore from being on the camel for so long. "While you're here, maybe you can answer some questions for me."

She shrugged. "Maybe, maybe not."

"The Fire God told me the people who raised me weren't my parents. Do you know who my real mother and father are?"

She pursed her lips. "I do."

I sat up straighter, my heart beating fast. "Who are they?"

"You're not ready for that. Next question."

I sighed, but tried again. "What am I supposed to do about my two mates who aren't interested in bonding with me?"

"How should I know? I'm not here for relationship advice."

Gods, she was impossible. "Why *are* you here?"

"To warn you."

The wind whipped at my hair, and I tucked it behind my ear. "Warn me about what?"

She leveled her steely gaze at me. "You may have noticed that you can sense Jasin through your bond now, and he can sense you in return."

"Yes. I assume that will happen with Auric too once we finish at the Air Temple."

"Indeed. They'll be bound to you, and through them you'll receive their magic. But they'll also be tied to your life force."

"What do you mean?" I asked.

"After you're mated your connection with them becomes

so strong that if one of them dies, you will lose their powers. But if you die, they will die as well."

Her words shocked me to my core. "All of them?"

"Every one that is bound to you, yes."

My throat tightened up. "What can I do?"

"Nothing, but it's not all bad. With each man you bond with you become harder to kill, especially since you take on their resistances. Right now you can't be harmed by fire, for example." She tilted her head. "Of course, that means the Black Dragon is nearly impossible to defeat without destroying her mates first. But I think I've said enough."

I jumped to my feet, my boots sliding in the sand. "Wait, I have so many more questions."

She pulled her hood low as she turned away. "You'll get your answers soon enough."

And just like that, she was gone.

31

KIRA

For the next three days our group continued through the endless desert, sleeping when the sun was high in the sky and continuing on through the evening when it was cooler. We had little time to talk at all with the sand whipping at us and the camels' movements making it hard to do anything but continue forward. By the time we camped we were all too exhausted and sore to do anything but pass out or grumble at one another. Brin was the only one who remained cheerful, and if it weren't for her guidance I knew we would have certainly gotten lost out there.

On the third day we finally spotted something in the distance: a tower that reached high into the sky and disappeared into the clouds hovering over it. Around it was a small lake surrounded by palm trees, a welcome oasis in the middle of the harsh desert sands. The setting sun behind the tower kissed the sky with gold, and I understood why the Air God's Dragon was that color now.

We rushed toward the tower with renewed vigor, bolstered by the thought that our journey was nearing its destination. Enva's words still worried at me, but there was nothing I could do except move forward.

As we neared the tower, Brin let out a startled cry. "The tower...it's been destroyed."

Huge chunks of the tower had fallen off and now surrounded the structure, which I was surprised was still standing with all the damage to it. Brin lowered her camel to the ground and then jumped off it and rushed inside a crumbling doorway, calling out for Nabi, the High Priestess we were supposed to meet.

My mates and I followed after her, and once we were inside the temple the destruction was worse. A large spiral staircase that must have led up the tower was now in ruins and impossible to climb. Everything inside had been smashed or turned to rubble, as though the place had been abandoned for years—except Brin had claimed to have visited only a year ago.

We found Brin kneeling in the corner of the rubble, holding her hands to her face as shudders wracked her body. I rested a hand on her shoulder, but then I caught sight of what she was crying over: a burnt, broken body that had a woman's shape, with four larger bodies beside her. My stomach twisted at the sight, and at the memories it brought back of my parents' deaths.

"Nabi," Brin cried. "Who did this to you?"

I had a feeling I knew.

A prickling on the back of my neck alerted me to something behind us. Two glowing yellow orbs moved through the dark corners of the rubble, and I grabbed Reven's arm to get his attention.

"We're not alone," he said, as he reached for his twin swords.

Darkness gathered and began to form a human-looking figure across the room, and I realized the glow came from its eyes. Thin shadowy arms that ended in sharp claws reached toward us as it began to glide across the floor.

"What is that thing?" I asked, backing away.

"It's a shade," Auric said. "Don't bother with your weapons. Like elementals, they can only be killed with fire, earth, air, or water."

A shade? I stared at the thing before us in disbelief. I'd heard stories about the ghosts trapped between this world and the next, but I never was sure they were real. Few people saw them in person and lived to tell the tale, especially since shades wanted nothing more than to consume your life force. And I had a feeling they'd want mine most of all.

Brin backed up behind us, holding her long, thin blade despite Auric's warning. "How can we stop it?"

"Stay back," Jasin told her. "We've got this covered."

He formed a ball of fire in his hand and Brin gasped, but I supposed there was no keeping the secret from her any longer. This was the only way to defeat the shade.

Jasin launched the fireball at the shade and burnt it up

almost instantly, but many more glowing eyes began to emerge from the shadows and from higher in the tower. They moved through the rubble in front of them as though it was nothing but air, their dark forms tapering off near the floor. Shades could turn invisible and insubstantial, making them deadly to most people. But we weren't most people.

Reven summoned shards of ice at the nearest shades, Slade gathered stones from the rubble and coaxed them to attack, and Auric blasted the shades with a tornado-like gust of wind. Jasin kept throwing fireballs and I conjured my own as well, though I hesitated before releasing them. What if my fire got out of control again?

Despite the men's efforts the shades soon surrounded us, and I couldn't believe how many there were. Eerie yellow eyes glowed from every direction, all fixed on me. One lunged toward Brin and she swiped her sword at it, but it simply passed through the monster's shadowy form. I threw a ball of fire at the shade and it sizzled and disappeared into a cloud of smoke, but there were still more coming.

The men worked together to fight the shades back, and I conjured fire whenever one slipped through and got too close to me or Brin. It was a lot like fighting the water elementals, except the shades had a cold, cruel hunger unlike anything I'd ever seen before, which terrified me in a primal way. These were the things that came for you in your nightmares, except they were real.

Another shade got too close and nearly reached Brin, but I shoved her out of the way and took it out with a burst of fire. Something slashed into me from behind that was both freezing and burning at the same time. Pain consumed me and I stumbled forward as I let out a cry, but then turned to blast the shade behind me as it lunged for me again with its claws. My knees gave out, and Slade caught me in his arms.

"Kira's hurt!" he called out.

The men formed a tight circle around me while the burning freeze continued down my spine, along with something wet. I reached back and found blood coming from the gash running along my back, which must have been from the shade's claws. Oh Gods, a lot of blood. A wave of dizziness washed over me and I would have collapsed if it weren't for Slade holding me up.

"Hang on, Kira," Slade said in his low voice that rumbled through my body. I rested my head against his chest as he carried me out of the ruined tower and into the darkening night.

"I'm okay," I managed to get out.

"Put her down here and I'll clean the wound," Brin said, as she rushed around us.

Slade set me down on my stomach and I closed my eyes as my face pressed against the cooling sand. I soon felt something soft press against my back, while I heard movement nearby.

"They're gone," Jasin said. "We got them all."

The men kept talking, but their voices blended together and I began to drift away. My back throbbed relentlessly, and I could only hope that my gifts from the Spirit Goddess would be enough to heal me.

3 2

JASIN

When Kira woke, I breathed a huge sigh of relief. Even though I'd felt her through our bond and knew she would live, it was still a comfort to see it with my own eyes. Especially since I'd felt some of her pain when she'd been injured.

The gash on her back had completely closed, though the skin there was still red and swollen. Her other mates and I had taken turns resting our hands on it in case our energy would somehow help her, though we weren't sure if it did or not.

"Jasin," she said slowly as she tried to push herself up with a pained expression. "What happened?"

"One of the shades sliced through your back, but Slade managed to get you to safety while we defeated them. You're mostly healed now, but you shouldn't move too much yet."

She managed to sit up, though she leaned against me. The tent over us flapped against the wind, and Auric had warned us there would be a bad sandstorm tonight. The others were currently moving our things inside the temple ruins now that it was empty, where we would be safer.

"I could have died," Kira said, clearly shaken. "And you too."

"We all could have. But we didn't."

"No, you don't understand." Her fingers wrapped tight around my wrist. "Enva visited me again the other night."

"She did? Why didn't you tell us?"

"Because I knew it would only make you all worry, and we needed to focus on getting to the temple." She drew in a ragged breath. "But I should have told you what she said."

I drew her closer against me. "What is it?"

"Once we're bonded, our life forces are tied together."

"Yes, like when you gave me your energy on the boat."

"Exactly. It's how I can share your powers as well, but Enva told me it comes with great cost." She closed her eyes for a moment before continuing. "If I die, all of the men bound to me will die as well."

I nodded slowly. "That makes sense. It also explains why the Black Dragon is always surrounded by some of her mates. They know if they lose her, they'll lose their lives as well."

"Jasin, what if I had been killed today?" Her grip on my wrist tightened and she spoke frantically. "You would have died too. And if I bond with the others, they'll all be tied to my fate. I'm not sure I can do this anymore."

"Yes, you can. This is your destiny, and we all know there are risks." I touched her cheek softly. "Besides, even without the bond losing you would be the death of me. I wouldn't want to live in a world without you in it."

"Maybe so, but the other men don't feel that way."

"They do. Auric certainly does. Slade and Reven do too, they're just afraid to admit it. But trust me, they love you as much as I do. How could they not?"

She looked up at me. "What did you say?"

I stroked her face as I gazed into her hazel eyes. "I love you, Kira. I've loved you since that first tousle we had in the forest and every day since."

The hint of a smile lit up her face. "I love you too."

I pressed my lips to hers, relieved to finally tell her how I felt and to hear her say it in return. The bond flared between us, confirming everything we'd said with a calm warmth.

Auric slipped into the tent. "Good, you're awake. How are you feeling?"

"Better," Kira said.

He settled in beside her and wrapped an arm around her waist. "I just explained everything to Brin. She took it pretty well, all things considered."

Kira nodded. "Is everyone else all right?"

"Yes, we're okay," Auric said. "Shaken up, but mostly by seeing you get hurt."

"Hard to believe there were shades in the temple," I said. "I didn't think they were real."

"Me neither," Kira said.

Auric's brow furrowed. "I've read about them in books, but never imagined I'd see one in person. It has to be more than a coincidence they were waiting for us, especially after seeing what happened inside that temple."

"Do you think they're working for the Dragons?" Kira asked.

"Perhaps," Auric said with a sigh. "The Dragons must have destroyed the temple and killed the High Priestess and her mates, though I'm shocked they would go to such lengths to stop us. Especially since they're all supposed to serve the Gods."

"I'm not," Kira said. "The High Priestesses serve the Gods, who've chosen us as ascendants. That means the priests serve us now and not the current Dragons."

"Which means all the people at the other temples are in danger too," I said.

"More reason to finish up here and hurry to the Earth Temple," Kira said, as she struggled to stand.

Auric placed a hand on her shoulder to hold her down. "Not yet. You need to rest some more. In the morning we'll find a way to the top of the temple, but not now."

Kira looked like she might protest, but then she settled back down. "Fine, we'll wait until the morning."

I almost pointed out that no matter how fast we rushed, we'd be unable to make it to the other temples before the Dragons did anyway. They could fly, after all. The other High Priestesses would likely be dead within days, while we would still be out here in the desert. But I kept my mouth shut as I helped Kira up and into the temple, while the sandstorm began to pick up around us. Slade and Reven both watched with concerned eyes as I tucked Kira into the makeshift bed we'd made up, and then she was instantly asleep.

I turned to the other men and said, "There's something you should know."

33

KIRA

When I woke again, I was inside the temple and nestled against Jasin's naked chest with my other mates sleeping nearby. I managed to extricate myself without waking him, though he tried to pull me tighter against him.

I slipped outside to relieve myself, where I found Brin sitting on a piece of rubble while she watched the sunrise. She glanced up at me with a weary smile.

"You're up early," I said.

"I've always been an early riser. I also had a lot to think about." She glanced over at me. "How's your back?"

I stretched and twisted, but felt no pain. "Seems to be completely healed now."

"Incredible." She leaned back as she gazed across the desert. "I never would have believed any of it if I hadn't seen you all fighting the shades. Now I understand why Auric didn't tell me from the beginning."

"If you'd like to return to Stormhaven, we would all understand. As you can see, our journey is very dangerous."

She sat up straight and met my eyes with a defiant look. "Definitely not. I plan to help you take down the Dragons however I can. I'm not sure how exactly I can help, of course, but I'm pretty resourceful. I'll find a way."

I couldn't help but smile. "Good, because I'm tired of being the only woman here, and I could use a friend by my side."

She jumped to her feet and embraced me in her arms. "I'd be honored to serve the next Black Dragon."

We chatted for a few more minutes before I headed back inside the temple. As soon as I stepped inside the crumbling archway, big, burly arms gathered me up, and I found myself pressed against Slade's muscular chest. His mouth came down on mine, and he caught my surprise with his lips. As he swept his tongue inside my mouth and kissed me hard, I slid my arms around his neck to pull him closer. I'd worried he would never want to kiss me again, and that he cared for me as nothing more than a friend, but the way he kissed me now told me otherwise—even if he wouldn't admit it out loud.

When he pulled back, he took my face in his hands and gazed at me like I was truly treasured. "Don't scare me like that again."

"I'll try not to," I said, breathless from his kiss.

He drew me in for another passionate kiss, before releasing me. "Now go and do what you need to do."

He gave me a short nod before walking away. I pressed a hand against the nearby stone to steady me, still shocked that had happened at all.

A soft chuckle behind me made me turn. Reven leaned against the wall, and I wondered if he'd been watching all of that. His black hair was slightly mussed from sleep, but his blue eyes were sharp. "He pretends he doesn't care, but he would do anything to keep you safe."

I moved toward him until we were only a breath away. "I know another man like that."

His eyes narrowed. "Except the difference is, I *don't* care."

I rested my hands on his chest. After Slade's kiss I was feeling bold, and I was ready to start taking things into my own hands with Reven too. "Liar."

"I've never lied to you."

"You're not lying to me. You're lying to yourself." I moved my hands up to grip the collar of his shirt and pulled him closer. "But it's okay, because I know you care, even if you don't."

I dragged his mouth down to mine and slid my tongue across his sensual lips until he parted for me. I kissed him with all of the desire and longing I felt every time we were together, even when he tried to remain distant and cold.

For a second I worried the kiss would be one-sided, but then Reven let out a groan and took control of it. He spun me around and pushed me back against the wall, his hands pressing against the stone on either side of me as his mouth devoured mine. He put his whole body into his kiss, and all I could do was be swept away by it.

When we broke apart, he practically growled, "That didn't mean anything."

I patted his cheek with a smile. "Keep telling yourself that."

He slipped away, while I walked further inside the temple with a lightness I hadn't felt in ages. Maybe there was hope for me and my two brooding mates after all.

I found Jasin and Auric waiting for me at the bottom of the ruined steps, both of them looking so handsome it made my heart skip a beat. They'd once hated each other, but now they were united as my lovers...and as friends.

Auric offered me his hand. "Are you ready?"

"Yes, but how will we get to the top? The steps have been destroyed."

"I'll fly you up," Jasin said.

I arched an eyebrow. "Is that safe?"

"I practiced flying discreetly while we were at the palace. I'm pretty good at it now." He gave me a cocky grin. "Trust me."

"We don't have any other option," Auric said. "It would take too long for Slade to repair the steps."

I reluctantly agreed to the plan and we moved outside, where Brin waited with Slade and Reven. She gasped as Jasin's form began to change and he turned into a great, winged beast with crimson scales.

"It *is* true," she whispered.

Jasin lowered himself down to the ground and spread his wings so I could get on. I hesitated at first, since I'd never ridden a dragon before, but then I was able to scramble onto his back. Auric followed me a moment later, wrapping his arms around me from behind. I gripped one of Jasin's hard scales for support and swallowed hard.

"Ready," I said.

Jasin leaped into the air and my stomach bottomed out at the sudden ascent. A great flap of his leathery wings brought us higher, and I held on tighter while the ground below us got smaller. To his credit, Jasin managed to keep us fairly level as he flew higher, and he did circles around the tower as he gained altitude.

Behind me, Auric let out a great whoop and spread his arms wide. "This is amazing!"

I wasn't sure about that, but the view of the endless desert around us was pretty impressive. Jasin climbed higher and higher and the ground below us shrank to the point where I could barely see the people below, and I began to wonder how just high this tower reached.

We burst into the clouds, where everything around us was white, and discovered the top of the tower had an open-air platform that awaited us. Jasin set down on the edge of it and lowered himself so that we could slide off his back.

Auric patted Jasin's side. "Nice flying. You truly have improved."

"Thanks," Jasin said, with a strange reptilian voice. "Remember what I taught you."

"Thank you, Jasin," I said, before pressing a kiss to the top of his snout.

"You're welcome," he said with a wink, before leaping off the side of the tower and vanishing into the clouds.

Auric took my hand and we slowly stepped across the cloudy, dream-like platform, until we came upon a bed that was ready for us. I'd encountered a similar thing in the Fire Temple, and knew the High Priestess here must have prepared it for us before the Dragons killed her. I said a small prayer of thanks to her, before turning to Auric. "It's time."

34

KIRA

I drew in a breath. "Before we do this, there's something I need to tell you. Enva came to me the other night and—"

Auric held up a hand to stop me. "It's okay, I already know. Jasin told us what she said while you were sleeping last night. I understand."

"Are you sure you wish to do this? You'll be bound to me forever. If I die..."

He took my hands in his and gazed into my eyes. "Kira, I've never been more sure about anything in my life. I love you."

His words swept away my worries and filled me with light. Even though I'd been upset with him and wasn't sure I'd be able to trust him again, I found that my heart had forgiven him and was ready to move forward. "I love you too, Auric."

"You do?" He let out a relieved laugh and then pressed a dozen small kisses to my lips while he talked. "I'm sorry for everything I did, and I promise you I have no more secrets. All I want is to be your Golden Dragon and to serve at your side."

I touched his face lovingly. "I want that too."

He swept me into his arms and claimed me with a passionate kiss. Together we moved toward the bed, slowly removing our clothing as we went, unable to get enough of each other. I'd been hesitant about bonding with Auric a few days ago, but now I wanted this more than anything.

"You're so beautiful," he said, as he lowered me onto the bed and began caressing my body. "And smart, and strong, and kind. You're everything I could have wanted in a woman."

My nipples hardened almost painfully at his touch. "Auric..."

"Shhh," he said, as he moved down my body, leaving a trail of kisses in his wake. His mouth touched me softly everywhere, all the places he'd learned made me gasp and sigh. In a few days he'd already become an expert at pleasing me.

But I'd waited too long for this moment already. Every time we'd shared a bed with Jasin I'd wanted Auric inside me too, and I was more than ready. I dragged him back up my body and found his lips, then wrapped my legs around him, showing him what I needed. He settled in between my thighs and I practically ached with want, desperate to feel him inside me. It was just the two of us this time, and everything was perfect.

As he slowly slid into me, his face looked almost pained. He filled me up inch by inch until he was seated fully within me, and then he pressed his forehead against mine and let out a ragged breath. "You feel incredible," he said, and then his mouth lifted into a smile. "Definitely worth the wait."

"I'm honored to be your first," I said. "But I'll go mad if you don't start moving."

He lightly stroked my cheek as he stared into my eyes. "Me too, but I want to savor this moment. We'll never have another first time together."

He lowered his mouth to mine and gave me a kiss that made my toes curl and my body tighten around him. With a soft groan, he began to slowly move in and out of me, and his long length seemed to completely fill me, touching me in places I never imagined. But then he rolled us over so that I was on top of him, making me gasp as the position pushed him even deeper.

"I want to see you ride me," he said.

I sat up and rested my hands on his chest, enjoying how full this position made me feel. His hands circled my waist as I began to move slowly, allowing my body to find a natural rhythm. He looked up at me with stormy eyes full of lust and love as his fingers tightened on my hips. All my hesitations and doubts vanished and were replaced by a deep sense of rightness, a feeling that Auric was mine just as much as I was his, from now until eternity.

Auric thrust up into me faster and harder, urging me on. I threw my head back and let passion take over as I rocked against him. His hands slid up my stomach to my breasts, which he cupped in his palms while slowly rubbing my nipples in time to my movements. Then he lifted himself up and took one breast in his mouth, making me moan as his tongue flicked across my hard bud. I slid my fingers into his thick golden hair as he sucked on the other breast next.

He fell back and I began to ride him faster, my movements becoming wild as I bucked on top of him, unable to control myself. The delicious friction was building between us, and I could tell by the way he groaned that he felt it too. He met my thrusts over and over, his fingers digging into my skin, and we moved together in exactly the right way to push me over the edge. My body clenched up around him as I gasped and cried out, pressing my hands against his chest while the orgasm rushed through me. Auric kept lifting his hips to mine and then he was gone too, calling out my name as he came apart beneath me.

A strong wind swept over us and whipped my hair across my face as we rode through our pleasure together. We began to lift up into the air and I let out a shriek as a tornado swirled around and below us, but Auric only laughed and pulled me down into his arms, kissing me with so much love that my fear drifted away while we flew higher into the sky.

Slowly the wind faded and we floated back down onto the bed. I ran a finger along Auric's neck and gazed into his eyes, while he smiled back at me and held me tight.

"We're bonded now," he said, his voice content.

"Yes, we are."

He drew in a deep, satisfied breath. "I've always felt out of place or unsure about my destiny. But not anymore. This...this feels right."

It felt right to me too. No matter what had happened in our pasts, we were moving forward together—with Auric as my Golden Dragon.

35

AURIC

After the most incredible experience of my life, Kira and I donned our clothes and made our way to the edge of the temple's roof while holding hands. Here a thin ledge jutted out into the sky, and if it weren't for my magic, I might have been terrified of falling to my death as we moved across it over the vast emptiness below.

Clouds swirled in front of us as we waited at the edge of the platform, and slowly they began to coalesce and form something solid. Within seconds the clouds became a vast body with a long neck and tail that filled up the entire sky. Great wings flared out above us, glowing golden under the filtered sunlight. Lightning flashed in the beast's eyes, while steam billowed from its fanged mouth. It was larger than the Dragons we'd seen before and more primal and cosmic, like something from a dream that you would barely remember when you woke in the morning. As if I blinked, the image might slip away from me completely.

This was the Air God's true form.

Kira and I fell to our knees while the Air God flapped his wings, sending clouds and wind swirling across the sky. Awe filled me, along with a strong sense of humbleness. I'd been chosen by the Air God and I hoped he would still see me as worthy of being his representative.

"Rise," he commanded, though his voice was like the wind whispering secrets in my ears. "You have served me well, while my other Dragon has turned against me. For that, I shall grant you three questions. Use them wisely."

Kira glanced at me with uncertainty, and I nodded at her. I knew what she wanted to ask, even if I had a dozen questions of my own.

"Can you tell me who my parents are?" she called out into the sky.

"You are descended from the Spirit Goddess herself," the Air God rasped. "She gave birth to the first Dragon using all of the Gods' seeds, and Black Dragon Nysa was born many generations later in that lineage. You are her daughter."

Kira's face paled. "I...I don't understand. She can't be my mother!"

"When the Spirit Goddess's descendant reaches fifty years of age she always bears a daughter, who will replace her when she turns twenty after the Gods choose four Dragons to be her mates. This is how it was done for centuries, but Black Dragon Nysa prevented this from happening, allowing her rule to continue. Until you were born."

Kira seemed at a loss for words, her mouth opening and closing, and I knew she must be in complete shock at learning our greatest enemy was her mother. But that was only half of what she'd wanted to know. I stepped forward and asked, "Do you know who her father is?"

"No, only that he is not my Dragon," the Air God said.

That ruled out Isen, but there were three other Dragons, and Kira could be descended from any one of them. Assuming her father was a Dragon at all, and not someone else. I'd always assumed the Dragons were infertile until I'd learned Calla was Sark's granddaughter. Perhaps they could only have children with normal humans?

Kira needed some time to recover, and though I had an entire journal full of questions for the Air God, we only had one question left—and there was one thing only he could answer. "Why did you choose me?" I asked.

"I chose you for your wisdom, independence, and discipline. I saw that you would be a good match for Kira and would strengthen those traits within her."

I bowed my head. "Thank you. I'll do my best to honor you."

"Your three questions have been answered," the God said, as he extended his wings. "Now prepare yourselves. Danger approaches, and I cannot get involved further."

With those words he dissipated into the air, becoming nothing more than a strong breeze and a wisp of cloud. I knew we should find a way down the temple to prepare for whatever this danger was, but Kira was so distraught I wasn't sure she could move yet.

"Are you all right?" I asked her.

She covered her face with her hands. "The Black Dragon...I can't believe it."

I gathered her into my arms and held her close as a memory resurfaced of the one time I had seen the Black Dragon. She'd been doing a rare tour of the four Realms and had shifted into her human form briefly to speak to my father. I'd only seen her from a distance, but her fiery red hair had been unmistakable. The same red hair that I ran my fingers through now as I comforted Kira.

Kira might not want to believe it, but I knew in my gut that it was true. The Black Dragon was her mother.

"What if Sark is my..." she started, her voice rough with emotion but unable to finish the question.

Before I could answer, a roar burst through the sky, and I spun away from Kira just in time to blast away a burst of fire that had been flying toward us. Red scales and sharp fangs emerged from the clouds above as Sark appeared over us.

"Get back," I told Kira, as I moved to protect her with my body and my magic.

But then something else moved out of the corner of my eye. I saw a flash of gold before something hit me hard in the chest and knocked me off the platform. As I fell to the ground everything went dark, and my last thought was that I'd failed Kira.

36

KIRA

"Auric!" I screamed, as he dropped out of sight and disappeared into the clouds. Though normally I knew Auric could use his magic to float, Isen had hit him with his tail so hard it seemed my mate had lost consciousness. I nearly dove off the tower and tried to save him, but the Golden Dragon hovered before me and snarled, with the Crimson Dragon at his side.

"You." Sark's eyes seemed to burn right into me. "I knew it was you all along. I recognized your stench." He closed in on me, his dragon form looming tall. "Grab her."

His gleaming red talons reached for me, but I blasted him with my new-found powers of air. He shook my magic off easily, though it distracted him enough that I managed to dart out of his reach and hide behind the bed. I shot a burst of fire at Isen next, but he flapped it off with his shining wings.

"There's no use running," Isen said, his voice slimy in his dragon form.

"Auric!" I yelled again, praying he was still alive. I couldn't feel him yet through my bond, but I reached out with my senses and found Jasin's presence. "Jasin!"

"Your mates can't help you now," Sark said. "It's time you came with us."

"Is it true?" I called out, choking back my fear and anger. "Is the Black Dragon my mother?"

"She is," Isen said. "And she'd very much like to meet you."

I shook my head, unable to accept it, or the thought that Sark might be my father. Was that why he had killed my parents and tried to hunt me down? Had those kind people stolen me away from the Dragons somehow?

The two Dragons surrounded me, using blasts of fire and air to keep me from being able to run, and even though I knew logically that I should be immune to both those elements I wasn't ready to test that theory yet. They got closer and closer, reaching for me with their deadly talons, and there was nowhere for me to go. They would capture me and take me back to the Black Dragon—my mother.

But then shards of ice flew at Sark's side and he reared back with a roar. Stones knocked into Isen at the same time, pushing him back. I spun around as another blood red Dragon burst through the clouds and soared toward us. This one had a familiar smirk on his fanged face, with Reven and Slade on his back. Jasin opened his mouth and let out a stream of fire, which blasted against Isen's chest, while my other two mates kept up their assault too.

And then another Dragon shot into the sky, faster than I'd ever seen one fly before. It burst up over us and gleamed bright gold under the sun, before swooping down and slamming into Sark, knocking him off the tower.

Auric had returned.

He flapped his shining wings and did a spin in the air, already flying as if he'd been born as a dragon and not a human, then dashed toward me. Sark had already recovered and began rushing toward me again. I swallowed my fear and ran at full speed for the edge of the tower and then leaped off it, using my new powers of air to help guide me onto Auric's back. I hit him with a hard thump and scrambled to grab onto his scales before I slid off his back, but then I was able to swing my leg around and sit like I'd done with Jasin.

"You're alive," I said, rubbing the scales on his neck. "Thank the Gods."

He let out a roar in response as he spun us around on shimmering wings. Now riding on my own Golden Dragon, I faced off against the two Dragons we were meant to usurp. Jasin hovered at my side with my other mates on his back, and together we launched a stream of magic toward Sark and Isen.

With the four of us working together it seemed as though our combined efforts might work to push the Dragons back, and we might even defeat one of them for good. But then lightning formed in the air around us, nearly striking down my two Dragons. Jasin dodged one lightning bolt but his wing was seared at the tip, and Slade had to grab Reven to keep him from tumbling off Jasin's back.

As the lightning kept reaching for us, Auric let out another roar and a tornado formed in the air around Sark, while Jasin opened his mouth and spewed fire at Isen. Reven and Slade assaulted the Dragons with ice and rock, and I added my own fire and air too. We faced the other Dragons without backing down, using our magic in concert to drive them away, until the lightning around us ceased. With shrill cries, Isen and Sark flapped their wings and retreated back into the clouds, disappearing as quickly as they'd appeared.

I sagged against Auric's back, exhausted even though we were victorious. He turned his head to meet my gaze, and I spotted his intelligence and kindness even in his new dragon form. He was Auric through and through, even as a dragon. Jasin swooped over to fly beside us, while Reven and Slade scanned the clouds for any sign of the other Dragons returning. Pride and love swelled inside me at the sight of my mates. Somehow we'd stood up to two of the mightiest Dragons in the world—and we'd won.

37

KIRA

When we were certain that the other Dragons were truly gone, Jasin and Auric circled the tower together as they flew down to the ground, where Brin waited for us with a nervous expression. As Auric's scaled feet hit the ground, she leaped on us to hug both of us at once, which was a bit awkward since he was still a dragon.

"Thank the Gods you're all right," she said. "What happened up there?"

"Sark and Isen wanted me to go with them, but we managed to fight them off," I said. I debated telling her what the Air God had told me about my parents, but now wasn't the time. Besides, I wasn't sure I could even speak the words out loud yet.

"Incredible." She patted Auric's scaled side. "You look great as a dragon, my friend."

"Thanks." Auric stretched his wings, admiring his new shining form.

"You should have seen him," I told Brin. "He flew like he'd been doing it his entire life."

"A benefit of being the Air God's chosen one," he said.

Jasin touched down, and Slade and Reven leaped off his back. My two Dragons shifted back into human form and then my four mates surrounded me and wrapped me in their arms, passing me from one to the other to hold me tight and cover my face with kisses. Love and relief filled my chest as I kissed and hugged them back. These were my Dragons, my warriors, and my mates. No matter what happened or what we uncovered, they would stand by my side.

"How did you know we were in trouble?" I asked Jasin.

"I felt your distress through the bond." He grinned at Reven and Slade. "The other two weren't excited about climbing onto my back, but they didn't need much convincing when I said you were in danger."

"Only because we knew you couldn't handle it on your own," Reven said, as he crossed his arms. He was back to his brooding self, though I knew he cared for me.

"We'll always protect you, Kira," Slade said, but then he made a face. "Even if it means flying again."

"Thank you," I said. "We couldn't have defeated the Dragons without all of us working together, but now we need to hurry to the Earth Temple. The Dragons know who we are, and they know we have two temples left to visit. They'll be trying to stop us any chance they can, and will no doubt be waiting for us to arrive."

"Good thing we can fly now," Auric said.

"Can you both fly all the way to the Earth Temple?" I asked, glancing between Auric and Jasin. "With all of us on your backs?"

"Do we have a choice?" Jasin asked. "We'll manage it somehow. Even with frequent stops to rest it will be faster than taking the camels back to Windholm and then getting horses."

Brin nodded. "I'll set the camels free. They'll be fine."

"Then let's gather our things and set off," I said, as I gazed across the desert in the direction of the Earth Realm. Another long journey was ahead of us, and at the end of it was my mother. I shuddered at the thought before I turned away.

Together we went through our supplies and bundled up everything we needed, then left the rest behind. Auric and Jasin became dragons again, while the four of us climbed onto their backs and loaded our things onto them. I wasn't sure how far they could fly with our weight on them, especially since they were both new to this, but we couldn't delay here either.

As we lifted into the air, I thought again of the Air God's words about how the Black Dragon was my mother. I hadn't wanted to believe it, but I felt the dark truth of it within me, no matter how much I hated the thought. I could only pray that I would never become like her...or like whoever my father was. And when the time came, I would defeat her and her Dragons, because though they may have birthed me, they were not my family. My first family was the one that

Sark had destroyed, and my new family was the group that surrounded me now.

We began to fly north in the direction of the Earth Realm, where I hoped to see Tash again, meet Slade's family, and bond with him at the Earth Temple. Our path wouldn't be easy, and even though we'd been victorious today, I knew we'd gotten lucky. To defeat the five Dragons we needed more than luck, especially since they knew where we would be heading next. We were going to need more allies, and though the King of the Air Realm was a good start, he wouldn't be enough—not when the Dragons had the Onyx Army and could control shades as well. We needed the Resistance on our side, along with anyone else we could find. But to get help, I was going to have to reveal who I truly was to the world. There would be no more hiding, not anymore.

I'd thought I could live my life in the shadows, but it was time to step into the light.

ABOUT THE AUTHOR

New York Times Bestselling Author Elizabeth Briggs writes unputdownable romance across genres with bold heroines and fearless heroes. She graduated from UCLA with a degree in Sociology and has worked for an international law firm, mentored teens in writing, and volunteered with dog rescue groups. Now she's a full-time geek who lives in Los Angeles with her husband and a pack of fluffy dogs.

Visit Elizabeth's website: www.elizabethbriggs.net

ALSO BY ELIZABETH BRIGGS